THE
BOOK
OF
LOVE

Also by Lynn Weingarten
The Secret Sisterhood of Heartbreakers

The

BOOK

of

LOVE

Lynn Weingarten

HARPER TEEN
An Imprint of HarperCollins*Publishers*

HarperTeen is an imprint of HarperCollins Publishers.

The Book of Love

Copyright © 2014 by Lynn Weingarten

Library of Congress Cataloging-in-Publication Data
Weingarten, Lynn.
        The Book of Love / by Lynn Weingarten. — First edition.
              pages   cm
        Sequel to: The Secret Sisterhood of Heartbreakers.
        ISBN 978-0-06-192620-4 (hardcover bdg.)
        [1. Love—Fiction.   2. Dating (Social customs)—Fiction.
3. Magic—Fiction.   4. Blessing and cursing—Fiction.]   I. Title.
PZ7.W43638Bo 2013   2012040091
[Fic]—dc23   CIP
                                                          AC

Typography by Sarah Nichole Kaufman
13 14 15 16 17 CG/RRDH   10 9 8 7 6 5 4 3 2 1

First Edition

For
Griff

ON BREAKING A HEART
The Book of Love, page 1181:

When you're breaking a guy's heart, it's important to remember to look him in the eye.

He might not understand at first. He'll think this is a joke or a dream. Surely he won't have seen this coming. But, of course, you did.

Tell him he is wonderful, that you are sure that he is just perfect for someone, perfect for the person who is perfect for him. When he asks you if you really mean it, don't turn away. Don't stutter. Don't blink. Don't give him reason to think back and wonder what if, what if, what if. It's only fair to dash all hope once you have what you want.

Look him in the eye for his sake. But mostly do it for your own.

If you can't see his eyes, how will you know when the tears begin to fall?

One

Picture it: blinking lights, glistening skin, dozens of bodies moving as one, and Lucy Wrenn in the center of the dance floor, shaking her hips to the beat. *Moonshine Party* was what the invitation had said. *Dress code: MOON LANDING.* So everyone dressed as astronauts, as space aliens, as cheese, or all in silver, and headed off to this gorgeous old theater.

The reason for the Moonshine Party was that Jack—eighteen years old, looked like a surfer, thought like a chemist—had been brewing up a big vat of it in the bathroom of the apartment he shared with some friends, and it had just finished, or ripened, or whatever it is moonshine does when it's ready. The invitation read:

COME DRINK PROFESSOR JACK'S LATEST EXPERIMENT.*
* It's already been tested, so we promise you won't go blind.**
** (probably)

The place could easily hold a thousand people, and on many nights it did, but on that particular night, there were just an intimate fifty, dancing, laughing, flirting under a high-domed ceiling from the center of which hung a huge chandelier, an entire planet of crystal and light.

Just then, the music changed from a fast thunking beat to something slow and slinky, and a guy who'd been trying in vain to get Lucy's attention decided to try a little bit harder. Robin was his name, and he was not important in the slightest, although he certainly thought he was. He was absurdly good-looking and had made the mistake of thinking that mattered a lot more than it did. Lucy knew he had a girlfriend but that he was there by himself pretending he didn't.

Robin leaned over. "What's your poison, sexy?" he said. Robin was the kind of guy who would hear a line in a cheesy movie, and then say it to a girl thinking he'd made it up.

Lucy acted like she hadn't heard him. He thought she was

playing hard to get. He didn't know she was impossible.

Lucy reached up and brushed her fingers over the tattoo that was peeking out over the top of her dress: a crimson heart, locked with gold, an aquamarine jewel-drop tear dripping off the point, and across the whole thing a violet ribbon on which had been inked *Secret Sisterhood of Heartbreakers*. She was one of them now and had been for the past six weeks. This meant many things—it meant she had broken a heart within the first seven days of having been dumped by her boyfriend, and she had brought the brokenhearted tear to a secret group of girls who used the tear's power to make her one of them. It meant now her heart was unbreakable and would be forever. It signified the fact that she could never again be sucked in by a jerk who didn't deserve her.

It also meant she was magic.

The tattoo was invisible to anyone who didn't have one herself, but at the party that night there were three people who did. Lucy's brand-new sisters: Olivia, Liza, and Gil.

Liza was on the opposite side of the dance floor with her arms snaked around the neck of a broad-shouldered tough guy, who was grinning like a fool. She was tall, with long streaky hair, a huge mouth, strong legs, smooth skin. Think of the word *luscious* and that's what she looked like.

Gil was over by the stage, brown eyes framed in a swoosh of silver eye shadow, short pixie hair spiked up. She was dancing with two skateboarder types, smiling and laughing as she did the moonwalk, the moon run, the moon shimmy and shake.

Off to the side, lounging in a big high-backed velvet chair, was Olivia, Lucy's third sister, platinum haired, high cheekboned, lightly freckled, calmly and coolly observing everything, the way she always did.

Lucy's and Olivia's eyes met, and Olivia winked, the corner of her mouth curling up. She smiled as if they shared a secret, because they did.

Next to Olivia, there was Pete, who was desperately in love with her and was the host of this party. Pete was from London and was handsome and fine featured in a way that made it easy to imagine him out in a field riding a horse. There was a rumor going around that he was a complete genius, had graduated from college at nineteen, and was now writing his PhD dissertation on some new field of sociology that he'd created himself, and his constant party throwing counted as research. This big old theater was his house, where he lived with his two roommates, Betsy and Caramellow, who were cats.

Seven weeks ago, Lucy had never met any of these people. But they were part of her world now, her brand-new life.

And there next to Pete was a piece of her old one.

Floppy hair, a little bit of face scruff, a sweet smiley mouth, and squinty blue eyes that made him look like he was always laughing. Tristan. From far away it would appear he hadn't dressed up at all, but if you got close to his feet, you'd see his gray Converse had been painted to look like the surface of the moon. Glued to the toe of one was a miniature rocket ship. To the other was an assortment of tiny aliens. He was leaning against the wall, slowly sipping a beer, and either didn't notice, or didn't particularly care, that there were three different girls appreciatively eyeing him from various parts of the room.

Tristan was Lucy's best friend, or at least used to be. That day it was hard to say for sure what Tristan was. This was the first time they'd hung out in the six weeks since Lucy had inadvertently found out he loved her and had accidentally broken his heart.

Lucy watched as a curvy girl in a sequin dress danced over to him. The girl leaned down to get a closer look at his moon feet. She stood up laughing. They smiled at each other. Lucy felt a rush of something. Hope, that's what it was. Hope that something would maybe start between him and this girl, or any girl, really. It was the secret reason she had invited him.

Lucy crossed her fingers as she watched them. Tristan looked up, saw Lucy staring, raised his beer, and tipped it toward her smirkily, a little joke about the kind of suave slickster who'd do that and mean it. And Lucy smiled at his mouth, his nose, his hair. She could not look him in the eye. Not anymore.

Everyone agrees it sucks to be in love with a friend who doesn't love you back. But no one talks about how hard it is to be the friend.

The girl was gone now. Tristan waved Lucy over, and she danced her way toward him.

"I LOVE your shoes!" Lucy shouted when she reached him. "You made those, right?! They're AWESOME!" She'd started overemphasizing everything, adding exclamation points to the end of every sentence, as though by staying relentlessly perky she could distract him from everything else.

"Thanks, bud," Tristan said.

Lucy pointed up to the ceiling. "Big chandelier, huh?! I hope it doesn't fall and crush us!"

"Looks pretty sturdily up there!" Tristan grinned. Tristan kept his feelings on the inside and dealt with this the way he dealt with everything—by joking, by smiling, by trying to make sure everyone else was having fun. He had no idea just how much Lucy knew.

Up on the stage, blue lights began to blink. "That's my cue," Lucy said. She felt a little flood of relief. She didn't know how to act around him, but more importantly, she had no idea how to help him.

"Go get 'em, tiger," Tristan said. And Lucy smiled and nodded and made sure not to look him in the eye so that for a moment, just a moment, she could pretend everything was okay.

Two

♥

Lucy smiled out into the sea of silver. "Ready, boys?" she said. She turned halfway around to check. Behind her, Jack was dressed like a space professor and holding a guitar. B was wearing a glow-in-the-dark alien T-shirt and holding a bass. In between them were two laptops, and off to the side a guy named Mica, who Lucy had never met before, was sitting behind a drum set, shirtless, wearing a silver Mylar blanket as a skirt. Apparently he always dressed like this.

Jack reached into his vest and pulled out a little sheet of paper with a rocket drawn on one side and a bunch of words on the other. "Lyrics, my dear Lucicle," he said, and handed the paper to Lucy. At the top was written *Things I'd Bring with Me to Space*, and Lucy smiled because, knowing him, it was less a song and more an actual list he'd made, y'know, just in case. *Tinfoil hats. Gravity mats.* Yes, Lucy thought, this would do just fine.

The first time Lucy was up on this, or any, stage was six and a half weeks ago, and it was the scariest moment of her life. It was the first time she'd ever sung in front of anyone other than Tristan. But she'd stood there with a thousand people watching her and closed her eyes and sung from the crack in her broken heart. Now her heart was solid as stone, and all her singing came from her shiny-glossed lips.

"Just make 'em sound pretty," Jack said.

And Lucy nodded. "Of course."

Here's a thing about Lucy, which she'd always sort of known, but felt weird admitting, even to herself because it seemed so braggy (although lately it had felt less braggy and more just *true*)—Lucy was a damn fine songwriter. Not just when she was playing by herself on her own guitar (which she hadn't done in a very long time) but when she was improvising with others. If someone was playing any kind of music at all, she could make up a song to go with it, right on the spot, that would emerge from her mouth fully formed and beautiful.

The music started, first quietly: the crackle of static, the tinkle of bells. Lucy stared out into the crowd. Gil was next to Tristan now, smiling up at him. She stood on her tiptoes to whisper something in his ear. Liza was a few feet away. "POP YOUR TOP OFF, HOTTIE!!" she shouted, and toasted Lucy with her little silver flask. Lucy just grinned and shook her head. And then she began to sing:

Tinfoil hats
Gravity mats
Astronaut bats
Schrödinger's cats

She went up high on the word *cats*, really belted it out from the center of herself. The crowd whooped and wooooed. She kept going down the whole long list. When she got to the line *And I'd bring a picture of you,* she lowered her voice, then brought it back up and rode a wave of clear falsetto right through to the final note. The crowd exploded, clapping, screaming. She could hear her sisters cheering louder than everyone.

Lucy stood there basking in it, basking only for a moment.

"Thank you, Lucicle!" Jack shouted.

Lucy walked offstage. She saw Robin trying to make his way toward her from across the room. As a Heartbreaker, Lucy knew this was the very sort of relationship she was supposed to be cultivating. She should have been thinking of him as less a creepy jerk to get away from, and more a creepy jerk who had a heart she could grab, squeeze, and juice the magic out of. But in that moment, all she cared about was going anywhere he wasn't.

The pumping dance music had started again, and Lucy headed back out on the floor, where Gil was laughing as Tristan spun her around and around. Lucy's eyes met his, and just for a split second, Tristan's smile faltered and Lucy saw what was underneath.

Lucy felt someone poke her in the side and then heard Liza's voice in her ear. "My offer still stands," she whispered. "I wouldn't even mind. He's hotter than I remembered."

The "offer" Liza was referring to was her offer to make out with Tristan. "Otherwise he's going to be mooning over you all night, pun intended," was what she had said earlier that evening as they got ready for the party. Less than two months ago, the idea of Liza making out with Tristan would have terrified her because she'd have been worried Liza would break his heart. Now it was way too late for that.

"I don't know," said Lucy.

"Well, it couldn't hurt," Liza said with a grin.

In a flash, Liza was standing in front of Tristan and was grabbing him by his sweatshirt hood strings and pulling him toward her. She danced in close, then drew her face right up to his and caught his lip between her teeth, as if she was taking a bite of a delicious dessert that she planned to devour every bit of.

"Daaaaamn." Lucy turned. Robin was standing right next to her now, holding two drinks. He let out a low whistle as Liza wrapped one gorgeous arm around Tristan's neck. "Sign me up for some of *that*!"

Tristan put his hands on Liza's waist, then slid them around the small of her back. Everyone around them was staring at them under the blinking lights—Liza's luscious curves, Tristan's tall lankiness. They looked, Lucy realized, beautiful together.

Lucy felt hot prickles on the back of her neck and deep in her belly. How weird it was to see Tristan actually kissing someone. He went out with plenty of girls, and although he wasn't a big kiss-and-tell type, Lucy wasn't stupid. Still, she had never once actually *seen* him kiss anyone in the six years they'd been friends. He looked good at it.

"Lucky guy," Robin said. She felt his hot breath on her ear, and she shook it off, shook him away.

The music slowed, and Liza and Tristan finally separated. Liza was smiling; Tristan just looked kind of bewildered, and not necessarily in a good way.

"Here," Robin said. He thrust a drink in front of Lucy. "I got you a girly drink." Lucy looked down at a bright red concoction with a straw, a strawberry, and a little paper umbrella poking out of it.

"Save it for your girlfriend," Lucy said.

"Who said I have one?" Robin looked away.

Lucy lowered her voice to a sultry purr, just barely audible over the thump of the music. "What's her name again?" She leaned in close. "I want to know whose boyfriend I'm about to hook up with."

Robin paused for a moment as though he couldn't tell if Lucy was kidding or not, his girlfriend's name resting unsaid on the tip of his tongue.

So Lucy reached into her purse for a small metal box, and poked around inside until she found what she was looking for. "Breath mint," she said. And she popped a Tip of the Tongue Tart between his lips. "You could use one."

For a moment he was silent. His eyes widened. "Stacy," he said. And then clamped his hand over his mouth.

Without another word, Lucy hooked her finger through one of Robin's belt loops and pulled him forward. She slid her hand into his pocket, pulled out his phone, and scrolled to the S's. And there was Stacy, a sweet-looking girl waving at the camera.

"What are you doing?"

Lucy held her finger up to her lips. "*Ssh*."

Lucy tapped TALK. "What the hell!" Robin shouted. He tried to grab the phone away.

Lucy turned. Robin reached around her. Lucy dodged him. Red drink sloshed on his shirt. After a single ring, a girl picked up.

"Oh, good," she said. She sounded so happy and relieved.

"I've been trying to call you all night!"

Lucy's heart pounded. She took a breath. "Hey, Stacy, listen, you don't know me and I'm sorry to be the one to have to tell you this, but your boyfriend is a dick. He's not at home with a cold, or out with the boys or doing whatever it is he told you he was doing instead of hanging out with you tonight. He's at a party trying to cheat on you. Just thought you deserved to know."

She locked eyes with Robin. He looked, for a moment, quite sick, then tried to smile. "I know you didn't really call her," he said.

"Didn't I?" said Lucy.

She turned the phone toward Robin so he could see the talk time ticking and hear the girl's shouts coming from inside the phone.

Robin opened his mouth in an O as the drink he had brought for her dropped to the floor, the liquid spreading out into a sticky circle.

Someone cranked the music, and Lucy walked away.

She saw Tristan standing against the wall, all alone.

Six weeks ago, Lucy made a silent promise to find him someone else to love, someone as funny and fun and sweet and brilliant as he was. But in that moment, Lucy suddenly understood with the force and clarity that only comes from finally facing a truth you've already known but have tried hard to ignore—finding Tristan a girlfriend wasn't the answer.

Lovers fight, leave each other, lose interest, get bored, cheat. Sometimes love is yanked away all at once, sometimes it simply leaks out drip by drip. Even the perfect love that lasts a lifetime ends with death. They say time heals all wounds, but the truth is time also breaks all hearts. *Every love ends in heartbreak.*

It's a scary, dangerous world out there for anyone with a breakable heart. It's only safe for those whose hearts are unbreakable. Like Lucy, like her sisters. They were the only ones who were truly free.

And standing there in that dark room under a high ceiling twinkling with crystal, dance music pounding in her chest like a heart, Lucy felt a stab of intense longing so strong it almost knocked her over. It was as strong as the longing she'd felt the moment she first saw her ex-boyfriend, Alex, who'd broken her heart. *This* was what she needed for Tristan—the freedom she had. *This* was how she could repay him. By finding a way to fix his heart forever the way he had helped her fix her own.

Of course this was the answer—it was amazing she hadn't realized this earlier. It was perfect. It was the only way to make things right.

Now all she had to do was figure out how.

Three

On Lucy's thirteenth birthday, her father gave her a shiny green bicycle with a million different gears. At the time, this gift only proved how little her father knew, and for the first two and a half years the bike sat at the back of the garage untouched; the only trips it ever took were a couple wobbly rides down to the end of the driveway. Lucy was not a bike person. She did not like riding down the road, always feeling so unsafe. She did not like that there were no straps, was no seat belt. She did not like how easily she could fly off.

Lucy relied on her parents for rides. Then after Tristan got his license, he drove Lucy anywhere she wanted to go and said he was happy to do it. He loved driving! (Now Lucy realized, actually, he'd loved *her*, but she didn't know that at the time.) When Lucy first met the Heartbreakers, Olivia would pick her up and drop her off. And when she needed her own transportation, she'd walk. But after a week of one-, two-, three-hour walks home from wherever the Heartbreakers had taken her, Lucy remembered the bike at the back of the garage and pulled it out. And suddenly it seemed like the perfect solution—a bike was sleek and simple, powered by nothing but gravity and gears, by her own muscles steadily sending blood through her veins and back to her impenetrable heart. She loved the freedom; she could go anywhere, didn't need gas or to ask anyone. When she wanted to think, she went for a ride. Her brain worked best when she was in motion.

So an hour later, the party winding down, Lucy climbed onto the seat in her gunmetal gray dress, strapped her silver helmet onto her head, and pedaled off into the night, imagining that to anyone who passed, she'd be nothing but a silver *whoosh*, like the tail end of a comet. She loved the feeling of going so fast she couldn't stop, of rushing down a hill at incredible speeds, of knowing there was real actual danger and that any second she could crash.

Lucy propped her bike against the side of the house and went inside. Her mother was sitting on the couch in the dimly lit living room. Lucy missed the clean scent of trees and crisp fall air rushing past her cheeks.

Right away, she knew they were fighting again. The usual evidence was all there: her mother had a full mug of tea in front of her but wasn't drinking it; the TV was on, but she wasn't watching it; and she was wearing a pair of faded blue and white striped pajama pants and a threadbare gray college T-shirt that she'd had since she was a student. She always wore it after a fight, as if she was trying to remind Lucy's father that she had a life before she met him and that she could have a life after. Even though, as far as Lucy could tell, her mother didn't really believe this.

"Hi, Mom," Lucy said.

Lucy's mother turned and gave her this blank, blinky, questioning look, not one that asked where Lucy had been and why she was coming home after one on a school night, but rather one of more global confusion, like nothing in the world made sense and she was hoping someone could explain it to her.

"What's going on?" Lucy asked because she knew she was supposed to.

Her mother took a breath. "Your father and I are getting a divorce." There was forced flatness in her voice like she was trying to sound as though she was just stating a fact. But Lucy knew her mother was saying this as much for her own benefit as she was for Lucy's. She just wanted to hear herself say it out loud.

The thing is, Lucy had had this same conversation at least a dozen times before, and her mother's words could not shock her. It was only her own words that did. "I hope you really do it this time," Lucy said. And both she and her mother looked up in surprise.

"What do you mean?"

Lucy ran her tongue along the roof of her mouth. The sour smell of the room had curled itself into her nose, and suddenly it was as though she could taste it. Her parents were a perfect example of love gone wrong, the way love always did. It had sunk its spiny hooks deep into their hearts, connecting them irrevocably together. No matter how much they seemed to want to separate, they couldn't quite manage. "Because you and Dad have been talking about this for years," Lucy said. "And maybe you'd both be happier if you just actually did it."

It felt good to be honest with her mother for the first time in a very long time. At least for a moment it did. But when Lucy looked at her mother's face, at her hurt expression, her own sure sense of calm was replaced by a stab of guilt. Her mother didn't want to know the truth, and it was not Lucy's place to try to force her to hear it. Lucy wished she were somewhere else, back at the party or out in the world. Not here with her mother in her pajamas and that sour smell.

"I'm sorry," Lucy said. "I shouldn't have said that." And she looked down.

"You don't give up on love." Her mother reached for her

cup of tea and held it in her hands but still did not drink it. "Maybe one day when you're older, you'll understand."

Lucy imagined just opening her mouth and letting it all spill out—telling her mother that she had already been in love and had her heart broken and now she was far beyond ever sitting on the couch staring silently into space over anyone ever again for the rest of her life. How wonderful it was to be done with that. But of course, she couldn't say any of this. "You're right, Mom," she said gently. "I'm sorry."

Their eyes locked again, and Lucy could see straight into her mother's heart. And no matter how big the rift was that had, in the last few months, sprouted in the space between them, Lucy couldn't bear to see her mother suffer.

Lucy had an idea. She reached for her mother's cup.

"Where's Dad?"

"He's up in our room." Her mother's voice caught on *our*. "I think he's awake. . . ."

Lucy nodded. She slipped her hand into her little purse and pulled out a tiny white star.

"Oh, look," she said. She motioned toward the clock on the wall. "One eleven, make a wish."

Her mother smiled sadly. "I think I'm too old for making wishes."

Lucy shook her head. "No, you're not," she said. "No one ever is."

When she looked down, the white star had turned to gold.

Lucy popped it in her mouth and crunched down.

I just wish he would talk to me, Lucy heard her mother's voice whisper. *I wish we could talk to each other and just be nice.*

Lucy took a breath. "I'll get you a new cup of tea," she said. "This one's gone cold."

She ran up to her room, closed the door behind her, and took the evergreen silk box from the back of the bottom drawer of her dresser. Inside was a tiny pot of crystals, a thimble-sized jar of lotion, and a clear vial with a miniature eyedropper containing a solution of heartbreak tears diluted 10:1. Lucy sprinkled a few crystals onto her palm and mixed them with a single droplet from the dropper. A wisp of smoke rose up into the air and formed itself into the face of a boy with a pointed chin, huge eyes, and a mean-looking mouth. Dove Marin. Lucy remembered seeing his name on the tear vial. Apparently he was some guy in a band whose heart Liza had broken the previous spring. Lucy silently thanked him, wherever he was, for making it possible for her to do what she was about to do.

Lucy put the case in the drawer and went back downstairs to the kitchen. She turned on the kettle and then went about preparing the mugs—a splash of half-and-half for her mother, two sugars and a lot of milk for her dad, and a tea bag and sprinkle of Sweet Talk Sugar for each of them. She walked back into the living room and set both mugs down on the table.

"DAD!" she called out. "Can you come downstairs for a minute? I made you some tea!"

Then she turned to her mom and whispered, "Just talk to each other, okay?"

By the time Lucy got back to her room, she could already hear the quiet murmur of their voices.

There was a time when this all would have made her so sad—hearing them get along after a fight was even worse than their fighting. She knew it wouldn't last. But this was her mother's wish. And so Lucy had helped. That was all.

Still it reminded Lucy of the vow she'd made earlier that night—the vow to Tristan and to herself, to spare him from his heartbreak, from all of this, really.

And she knew it would take a lot more than a little Wish Star to fix that. Lucy took out her phone. She typed: *Can you meet me after homeroom tomorrow at the big tree out front? There's something important I need to ask you. . . .*

Then Lucy got into bed and closed her eyes, and to the sound of her parents' hushed laughter, she drifted off to sleep.

Four

I t was 7:45 in the morning, and Lucy was walking down the halls of Van Buren watching the dancing lines of light. There was a strawberry stripe between a girl who was holding hands with her boyfriend, and his best friend who was waving at them from across the hall. There were rose-colored streams passing back and forth between two shy freshmen, too scared to look up from their phones. There was a ruby shimmer stretching between two players on the football team, both walking with their arms around their girlfriends.

When Gil had taught Lucy how to make the Love Lines potion a couple weeks back, she'd explained that the lines you saw after putting the drops in your eye didn't always signify love that currently existed—the lines also indicated love that *could* be. Where the line started was the lover, and where the line pointed was the lovee. If the line stretched both ways, the two people either were in love or one day might be. Potential. That's what the lines showed.

The potion only worked for a few hours per dose, but today Lucy had a hunch, and if her hunch was right, then a plan. And it would take only seconds to figure out what she needed to know.

Now there was a line starting at the heart of an angry-looking girl in an oversized brown sweater pointing toward a beautiful boy in a bowler hat, and one from his heart, stretching right back to hers. Lucy reached up and gently plucked the line of light like a string on a guitar. The two of them looked at each other. And that was where Lucy left it; today she had other things on her mind.

Lucy walked to her homeroom, sat down, and looked around at her fellow W's, staring down into their book bags and at their homework and breakfasts. W for Wrenn.

W for Wishmaker.

The morning after she became a Heartbreaker, Lucy realized something—breaking hearts was the method by which one got the magic. But once you had the magic . . . that's when things really got interesting. Lucy was a Heartbreaker now, and so officially what she did was break hearts. But unofficially what Lucy had been doing was something else entirely.

Lucy turned toward Jessica Wooster, whose puffy blonde hair was puffing out around her pink face, like a lemon meringue balanced on top of a strawberry. Lucy felt a kinship with this girl for reasons she wasn't quite sure of—maybe because she always looked so far away, like she was imagining herself somewhere else. The way Lucy used to before here became better. Lucy wanted to help her. Maybe today she could.

Last Friday during homeroom Lucy had turned to Jessica at 7:47 and said perkily, "Ooooh, seven forty-seven! Time to make a wish!" And Jessica had stared at Lucy as though trying to decide whether this was Lucy's confusing way of making fun of her somehow and/or if Lucy maybe had something slightly wrong with her.

"No, seriously," Lucy had said. "Seven forty-seven is supposed to be a really lucky time. I read it in my horoscope this morning." And Jessica had just smiled, clearly deciding on option two, and turned back toward the front of the room. *But not before making a wish of her own.*

When Liza had taught Lucy about the stars, she had explained that a Wish Star only worked when wishes were consciously made. "Get him to make it on an eyelash, a blown-out birthday candle, a necklace with a clasp at the front, what*ever*," Liza had said. "So long as he actually thinks it." Then Liza had gone on to explain that once you knew what he wanted, you didn't give it to him, but rather figured out a way to dangle it in front of him. "Always leave him wanting something," Liza had finished.

But Lucy had another idea of what she could do with the Wish Stars: She could listen to people's wishes. *And then she could make them come true.*

Big wishes were out of her league, of course—she couldn't make anyone famous or rich, she couldn't make anyone taller or shorter, she couldn't make boobs shrink or grow, she couldn't cure anyone's sick loved one (although hearing wishes like that was awful). But every so often someone wished for something small—to be able to make a single basket in gym class while their crush was watching, to once, just once, have the perfect comeback to a bully right when they needed it the most. These wishes Lucy could actually help with. And so she did.

For example, last month in bio, Lucy dropped a glittering little pellet into Angeline Strathmore's mango juice, and then for the first time that anyone could remember, the girl got through an entire oral presentation without looking like she was going to vomit from nerves.

And the week before, in European history, when Kevin Marx and his gang of jerk friends were tossing bits of tuna sandwich at Dougie Fishman's head, they suddenly felt all of their insults bounced back on them tenfold. Of course, they couldn't see the invisible Rubberglue Bubble Lucy had blown around Kevin, but they could definitely feel its effects. Within three minutes, one had left for the nurse, claiming a headache, one's lower lip started trembling as he quietly brushed back a tear, and Kevin himself, red with embarrassment, stared silently down at his desk for the rest of the class. They'd left Dougie alone since then.

Last Friday, just as homeroom ended, Lucy had popped Jessica's Wish Star in her mouth. As she bit into it, she heard Jessica's voice whispering in her ear, "I wish that he would love me." Lucy knew that love only led to heartbreak, but she had committed herself to granting wishes, not telling people what their wishes should be. Of course, Lucy did not know for sure who *he* was then, but she had a hunch.

And now, standing in homeroom, magic had confirmed it. From the center of Jessica's light green T-shirt shone a line of light—delicate, petal pink, so faint Lucy had to squint to see it. Lucy followed the line straight to the center of the chest of the guy in front of her, Jason Walser. Jason with his hair hanging in his face, playing imaginary bass guitar in his lap, occasionally taking bites of his peanut butter sandwich, was completely unaware of anyone around him, but there was a line coming out of Jason's chest too, a faint pomegranate stripe that stretched right back to Jessica.

Ms. Eamon was up at the front calling out names. And as

the room filled with "here" and "yup," Lucy smoothed a dab of almond-scented Empathy Cream into each of her palms, then poked her finger into the tiny secret pocket of her bag and fished out a steel capsule the size of a vitamin pill. "For emergencies only" is what Olivia had said when she gave it to her.

Well, what's high school if not one long one?

Locked inside that steel was an undiluted heartbreak tear. This one was from Scott, the bouncer with the giant muscles and propensity for writing earnest love poems, whose heart Liza had recently broken. *Thank you, Scott,* Lucy whispered as she unscrewed the top. She dumped the tear onto the tips of her fingers and pressed them together.

Usually diluted tears were used to activate the magic in whatever potion or elixir one was using, but with the help of a Heartbreaker as conduit, an undiluted tear could dissolve the barriers between hearts. Lucy wouldn't be creating feelings that didn't exist, but rather opening up a pathway for those that were already there.

Lucy stood up and walked forward.

"Hi, Jess."

Jessica tipped her head to the side. "Hey, Lucy," she said. She smiled slightly.

"That's a pretty bracelet," Lucy said. "Let me see. . . ." She reached out for the thin beaded band and pressed her thumb to Jessica's wrist like she was taking her pulse. In less than a second, Jessica's feelings flooded her—a rush of confusion, a prickle of nerves, and a surge of fierce bravery. Jessica was ready for her life to change. Lucy smiled. Well, change it would.

"Jason," Lucy said. "What size are your wrists? Let me check." She knew she sounded stupid, but she didn't even care. In a second, he'd forget all about her anyway. Lucy could feel his heart pounding, and his feelings right after, so similar to Jessica's—the confusion, nerves, a slight hint of wonder. Their hearts beat under her thumbs. Lucy took a deep breath and concentrated on pulling up the energy from the center of the earth—through the rock, the soil, the floor of the building, up through her legs, into her chest, and out through her fingers. Lucy closed her eyes and behind her lids watched quick flashes of images of the two of them together—Jason brushing Jessica's hair from her cheek, Jessica leaning her head against his shoulder, him playing a song for her, her handing him a gift, the two of them locked in an embrace, their lips meeting and parting and meeting again. These images were coming from them, not Lucy, although she could not be sure which was from who. She let them travel across her like a bridge, his passing to her, hers passing to him. She held them both there until she felt their hearts beating in sync. Then Lucy let go and stepped back, watching as they turned toward each other. Their eyes met, and in unison they took a breath. Jessica blushed. She looked down at the container of cottage cheese on her desk, then back up at Jason, who was still staring at her. He brushed his hair out of his eyes, and his lips spread into a smile. Jessica smiled back. And Lucy thought about what a lovely, lovely thing it was to watch someone get exactly what they wished for.

But she did not stay to see what happened next. The bell had rung and homeroom was over. The rest was up to them.

Five

Gil was waiting for Lucy under the big tree, just where she promised she would be. The sunlight was streaming through the branches, and her face glowed like someone in a commercial for face wash, or the after picture in an ad for antidepressants. She was sipping from an enormous cup of coffee.

Lucy approached, her stomach a jumble of nerves. When Gil caught her eye, she grinned. "So I've been testing out a new theory about half-and-half," Gil said. "And how you can never have too much of it." Gil handed Lucy the cup. "I think I may be onto something here."

Lucy took a sip of coffee. It tasted like hot coffee ice cream.

She handed it back. "You sound like Tristan," Lucy said. And at the sound of his name, her insides clenched.

"Did he have fun last night? Pete and the boys thought he was a hoot. They wished he'd stayed later, but he left right after you did."

"I don't know." Lucy took a breath. "Actually, that's sort of what I wanted to talk to you about."

"What's up?"

"Tristan's heart," Lucy said. "I broke it, which you already know, of course."

Gil nodded.

"But what I'm wondering is . . ." Lucy closed her eyes so she wouldn't have to see Gil's face when she asked her. She let the words tumble out. "Can we fix it? Fix his heart, I mean. And then give him an unbreakable heart like we have?"

For a moment, they were both silent.

Lucy opened one eye, then the other. Gil's head was tipped to the side, her expression unreadable.

Lucy looked down. Her whole body was tingling. "I don't mean make him into a Heartbreaker or let him do magic. We wouldn't even have to tell him what we were doing. I just don't want him to suffer like this. Not now or ever again." Lucy felt a prickling behind her eyelids, the kind that came when she was about to cry. But the tears didn't come. What was the point of having powers if those around you were still in pain? What was the point of any of this if the people you cared about most were miserable?

When she looked back up, Gil had that same peculiar expression on her face. She leaned in slowly. "I'm supposed to say no," Gil whispered. "I'm supposed to tell you that it's not possible. And that even if we ever *had* magic that powerful, we'd never 'waste' it on something like that. But . . ."

Gil stopped. She was suddenly all smiles, staring at a spot behind Lucy. "Hey there," she called out. "I was just telling our friend Lucy here how fun it was to have you at the party last night. . . ."

Lucy turned and there was Tristan, walking along, the sun in his face. He was grinning, just like he always was. But there were circles under his eyes. He looked tired.

"Party, you say?" He scrunched up his mouth and tapped his chin. "Hmm, I think you must be mistaken, Miss Gillian. I did not go to any parties last night. I retired at a reasonable hour, had a dream about a moon landing, and woke up with some glitter on my face. Same old, same old."

Gil laughed, then handed him her coffee. "Finish it," she said. "Those moon-landing dreams can be exhausting."

Tristan smiled at Lucy from behind the cup.

"Hello, buddy," he said.

"Hi," said Lucy. She smiled back and tried to think of something else to say.

But a moment later the bell rang, and she was spared.

The three of them started walking toward class, Tristan

a few steps ahead. Gil linked her arm through Lucy's and pulled her in close. "I'm *supposed* to say no," Gil whispered. "But there may be one tiny little chance. After all, we have magic on our side, which means . . ." Gil waggled her eyebrows.

Lucy felt hope bubbling up in her chest. She'd heard her sisters say this line before. "Anything's possible?" Lucy finished. She bit her lip.

Gil nodded, then winked. "Everything is."

Six

Lucy pushed open the door to photo class, and the sickly sweet smell of chemicals rushed out to greet her. Mr. Wexler was up at the front, leaning back in his black desk chair, reading a newspaper. "KEEP ON KEEPIN' ON" was written on the board in big block letters. When anyone walked in, he'd point to the board without looking up. This meant they were supposed to go back to whatever they'd been working on last class so he could read in peace. Lucy grabbed her film and headed into the darkroom, where the red light wrapped around her like a blanket. Gil's words were still echoing in her ears. *There may be one tiny little chance.*

Lucy found an empty enlarger between a cute junior

guy who gave her a shy smile and a freshman girl who was developing pictures of her own cleavage. Lucy put a strip of negatives under the enlarger and projected an image onto a sheet of photo paper.

She counted to seven, then took the paper and swished it in the vats of chemicals one after another, dropped it in the water bath, and walked out to the light side of the room. She fished the photo out and stared at it—there was Olivia in the driver's seat of her convertible, jaw set, staring straight ahead. Beside her, Liza was pursing her lips and checking her lipstick in the rearview. It looked like a fashion shot from a magazine. Lucy never could have taken that picture even two months ago.

When she first started taking photos, she'd wait until she got that *ping*-y feeling in her gut and snap a picture of whatever was the source of it. Now she was more skilled at operating her camera, for one thing, but also more deliberate. The *ping* came much less often; she relied on her eye and she shot what was pretty. And what was wrong with that?

Lucy stared at the photo again and felt a little jolt of pride. Not because of its quality, but because of the girls who were in it, the fact that they were her friends now, her sisters. When she took this photo, they were waiting for her to get in with them.

"Nice shot," someone said. It was Alex, standing next to her now. There was a time when his mere presence would have made her heart thud in her chest, her face flush, her whole body vibrate from his nearness. Then she only felt annoyed.

"Thanks." Lucy didn't even bother turning toward him.

All summer long, Lucy had spent nearly every moment of her waking hours thinking about this boy, who at the time had been her boyfriend. She wrote songs for him, and sent him presents and letters, looking giddily, breathlessly forward to his return. Then Alex came back from his summer in Colorado and promptly dumped her. And everything changed. Lucy now knew that while she had been pining away for him, he had been secretly seeing someone else.

"How are you?" His voice sounded tight.

"I'm fine," she said. And she raised her eyebrows. They were not anything resembling friends. They had pretty much avoided each other until now.

"Look, I have to ask you something," Alex said. "This is going to sound stupid."

She finally turned. "What's up?" He was looking at his shoes.

"When we were together . . ." He paused and took a breath. "Did you . . . did you think I was a bad kisser?"

Lucy wasn't sure if she should laugh or just turn and walk away. "Wait," she said. "Are you seriously asking me this?"

He was starting to blush. "Well, I was just wondering. . . ."

"You were fine, I suppose," she said slowly.

"And . . . and did you think I was a good boyfriend?" He was practically whispering now. What the hell was going on?

"Well, not particularly," Lucy said. And it was the truth, even discounting the way it had ended. He'd been self-centered and narcissistic. He hadn't ever really listened to her. He assumed she liked whatever he liked, and yeah, she played along with that and that was her own fault. But still. This was probably the most interest he'd ever paid to her opinion about anything.

"But you really liked me at the time, though, right?"

Lucy felt her insides growing hot. What gave him the right to ask this, to ask *any* of this? "What is all this about?"

Lucy looked at him more closely, and that's when she noticed the blotchy skin, the puffy eyes. Had he been . . . *crying*?

Suddenly Lucy realized what must have happened. "She broke your heart, didn't she," Lucy said. But it wasn't really a question.

Alex's eyebrows shot up. "She who?" He was trying to sound casual.

"The girl you were seeing over the summer," Lucy said calmly, as though Alex's love life was something they always talked about.

"I wasn't seeing . . ."

Lucy waved her hand. "Oh, please, Alex." She never said his name while they were dating. Somehow it felt both too personal and not personal enough. Now she said it like it was an insult. "It doesn't even matter anymore anyway, so there's no point in lying about it."

Their eyes met, and for perhaps the first time ever, they understood each other perfectly.

"I never meant . . . when I left for the summer, I didn't plan on doing something like that."

"I know," she said.

Alex took a breath. "I met her in the middle of a thunderstorm," he said. "It was one of those crazy ones that no reasonable person bothers trying to go out in." He looked to the side, eyes unfocused, totally in his head then. "I was at the cabin by myself, just thinking about some photos I wanted to take down by the lake the next day, and I looked out the window and there was this girl running by. At first I thought something was wrong, because why else would she be out in that? Turned out she was just dancing in the rain like some . . . I don't know what. And then the lightning started, and I went outside and said if she needed a place to wait until the storm was over, she could come in and . . ." Alex looked up then. "She did."

Lucy tried to keep the tiny smile off her face. Despite the fact that he was kind of an idiot for telling her all of this unprompted, she was more interested than Alex could have imagined for reasons he never could have begun to understand. The girl Alex had been cheating with was another

Heartbreaker, a fact that Lucy had only discovered by accident when looking at a photo Alex had taken of the girl—she had the Heartbreaker tattoo, which only showed up in the picture once Lucy herself had one. When she'd asked Olivia about it, Olivia hadn't known anything. "Just a lucky coincidence, I guess," Olivia had said. "We get around." Then she'd smiled. "Good thing, though, I guess. It means he'll get his." And she'd left it at that. Lucy knew it didn't matter anymore, but she couldn't help being curious.

"Go on," Lucy said.

"So she came inside and she was wearing this little sundress and it was all wet and like . . ." Alex's face turned pink right up to the tips of his baby-sized ears, which she used to love so much. "I gave her a towel to dry off. But she just patted her face and stood there staring at me, standing there in this wet dress. And she had this smirk on her face and said, 'Well, who knew you'd be this yummy.' Then she dropped the towel and grabbed my hand and pulled me outside. The lightning was crazy, and I was actually kind of wondering if we were going to get electrocuted." Alex looked up shyly, like a little boy. "I'm used to being the adventurous one, you know? Like the one who isn't thinking about the safety of a thing. But she just didn't give a crap. She made me dance with her, right there in the rain. It was, I don't know . . . it was unlike anything I'd ever experienced. It felt like magic."

Lucy nodded. The poor boy had no idea just how close he was to the truth.

They say love changes you. But maybe it's heartbreak that really does. The Alex standing in front of her with tears in his eyes was a different person than the one she had known.

"Exactly when did all that happen?" Lucy asked. But she didn't need to wait for him to answer. "It was the second night, wasn't it?"

Lucy was flooded with memory. The first night Alex was away, she'd spent hours doing nothing but waiting to hear from him. She wouldn't even take a shower, in case he called then and she missed it. But all she got was a single text around midnight. *Long trip. It's awesome here. Great photo-taking opps.* She tried calling him right after, but it went straight to voice mail. "Just wanted to say glad you made it there okay," she'd said. She'd rerecorded the message three times until she could stand the way her voice sounded.

The next day Lucy woke up queasy and anxious. She felt like he was so far away already, almost as though he was someone she'd imagined or made up. It was impossible to believe it had only been two days since she'd been kissing him good-bye. She'd reread every text message he'd ever sent her, and then she'd looked up the weather where he was in Colorado just to try and feel closer to him. When she saw that there was a tornado warning that day she'd felt worried for him but also weirdly relieved, because this gave her a good excuse to call him again. Somehow at the time it hadn't occurred to her how wrong it was that she felt like she needed an "excuse" to call her own boyfriend.

"Um . . . yeah, that was the night."

"Was she there when we talked on the phone?"

He nodded. He looked guilty. "I didn't pick up at first because it felt weird to while she was there, even though nothing had happened or anything. I just thought it would be awkward to try to explain it."

"To me or to her?"

Alex reached up and scratched the back of his neck. "Both, I guess. I was going to just try you back later, but you called and called. . . ." Lucy felt a prickling embarrassment for that other Lucy, the one who kept hitting the little green phone icon, four times in a row in fact, somehow unable to stop herself. She had had this strange and crazy jolt of worry when she couldn't reach him the first time. It wasn't because of the storm, even—the news said it was very mild. But rather this absurd and ridiculous feeling she couldn't shake, that somehow in between when she'd last spoken to him and then, he simply stopped existing.

Ahead of time she'd written out a little list of things they might talk about—a very cute and friendly three-legged dog she'd seen on her street, the movie she'd gone to about mountain climbing (which she only went to because Alex liked it), and hey, by the way, what exactly did he think of hedgehogs as pets?

When he'd finally picked up, she'd felt her body flood with relief. But things got awkward quickly. Their "hey"s and "how are you"s overlapped and kept overlapping, and she could barely hear him anyway over the sound of the rain. The call was short. She hadn't even gotten to bring up a single item on her list before he said, "Well, I won't keep you." Even though that was all she'd ever wanted.

She vowed that she'd let him call her next time. And so she devoted herself to taking pictures, to sending him presents, to waiting to hear from him. And wait she did. He texted every few days and sent an email here and there. Deep down she knew something was wrong, but she so didn't want to believe it that she spent the entire summer trying to convince herself not to trust herself. It was an exhausting mistake.

"After you and I hung up was the first time we kissed," Alex said. And she could tell by the rasp in his voice and the look in his eyes that Lucy's presence was now completely irrelevant to this conversation. He just wanted to hear himself talk.

"So what's she like?" Lucy said.

"She's like . . . she's just not like anyone else," Alex said. "She's completely fearless and spontaneous and crazy. When I asked her to come and visit me, she just hopped on a plane like it was nothing."

"She's here now?"

Alex nodded.

"Staying at your parents' house?"

Alex shook his head, then looked embarrassed. "No, at a hotel. I'm paying for it, though. She asked me to find one for her when I asked her to come. I was excited about it. I thought it was just so that we'd have a place to be alone to . . ." He trailed off.

"Have sex?" Lucy finished. She'd assumed they had already done it, that he had lost his virginity to her, both from the way he'd acted when he got back and from that picture she found. Still, it was weird to hear herself say it, to hear herself say it and have almost no feeling about it at all.

"Um . . . yeah," he said. "I guess." He turned away. "But I think she just wanted somewhere else to go so that she wouldn't have to stay with me after she dumped me."

"Hmm," Lucy said. "Weird." She did not like the way that she sounded now, so pinched, and sharp, and mean. She did not like the tiny smile she felt playing on her lips.

Alex looked so sad.

Lucy took a breath. Heartbreaker or not, she was still a human being. And the human response to someone's suffering should never be *joy*, no matter how much of a jerk that someone might be. "It's too bad that happened to you," she said gently. "Having a broken heart sucks."

"Thank you," Alex said. And then tipped his head, as

though something had just occurred to him. "Hey, so I was giving you space before because I thought I should or whatever, but you're clearly okay so . . . does that mean we can be friends now?"

Lucy paused. "Sure," she said. "Of course we can." But she didn't mean it.

Lucy walked back to the photo closet, went to her cubbyhole, and took out her contact sheets of the pictures she'd taken over the summer. She hadn't even glanced at them in weeks, not since she'd become a Heartbreaker. How funny to look back and see the world through the eyes of the girl she used to be. The pictures she took now jumped out and grabbed you. These old ones whispered your name over and over until you noticed.

She stared down at the row of tiny photos. In the center of the page was one of Tristan in profile, playing harmonica in his car as the sun went down. Lucy remembered that day, how the two of them had sat there, their feet up on the dash, eating Popsicles until it was black outside. What was special about the photo wasn't the composition or the lighting or any of that crap—what stood out was the look on Tristan's face, in his eyes. There was just so much of *him* in there—his sweet, funny, smart, weird self. She hadn't known why she was taking the photo at the time, just that something in her gut told her to.

She looked up at Alex, who'd just emerged from the

darkroom carrying a close-up of a crying eye. His eye. He held up the print, and rubbed his chin, like he was deep in thought about it. Then he glanced at Mr. Wexler, backed up toward his desk, and let out a cough. When Mr. Wexler didn't look up, he coughed louder. It was so obvious what Alex was doing that Lucy almost had to laugh—he was trying to get Mr. Wexler to notice his picture so he'd call the class over to discuss how great it was. Mr. Wexler had done it a few times for Lucy's photos, and Alex always looked so surprised, so shocked, that the compliment had been given to her and not him.

Lucy rolled her eyes and turned away. Perhaps he was the same old Alex after all.

Sometimes the world just made no sense. How was it possible that she'd fallen in love with this idiot—that she'd pined away for him, given him her heart, and let him break it? Yet *she'd* broken the heart of her best friend, the best person she'd ever known. It was completely wrong.

What mattered now was only this: Could she fix it?

There may be one tiny little chance, Gil had said.

Lucy just hoped it was enough.

Seven

illy, Rowan says he's buying you a ticket to visit him in Australia," Olivia said, reading from Gil's phone.

"Well, that's sweet," said Gil.

"Wonder if you can cash it in for the miles?" Liza said with a smirk.

It was later, school had just ended, and the four girls were sitting in Olivia's car, going through the day's collection of texts from flirting, lovesick, and heartbroken boys.

Lucy looked down at Liza's phone. "Jeremiah says he baked you cookies, although based on this photograph, I'm not entirely sure it would be advisable to eat them."

Liza let out a snicker, then stared at Olivia's phone. "Rick grafittied 'I love Olivia' on a bathroom wall somewhere in Canada. *Ooooh,* that naughty boy is committing *crimes* for you, Livvy."

Olivia shook her head. "Well, Aiden wants to know when Gilly's coming over to pick up the present he got her." Olivia reached back with the phone open. On the screen was a picture of a guy with a bow stuck to the top of his head.

"Tim says he can't wait to stare into your beautiful green eyes again," Lucy said. "And Craig S says you're hot."

Liza snorted. "Well, at least one of them's observant."

Olivia's phone buzzed. "Olivia, it's from Pete," Liza said. She cleared her throat and in a terrible British accent read, "'I had a dream about you last night, love. And yes, *that* kind of dream. I promise to tell you all about it later if you promise to act it out in person next time I see you. Also, when are you going to break my heart already, O-livia? I've been ready for ages, you know.'" Liza turned. "Okay, fine, I added that last part myself. But seriously. When are you going to do it?"

Olivia shrugged. "What does it matter? It's not like we're lacking in tears."

"I have one more for Lucy," Gil said. "From Colin."

At the sound of his name, Lucy's stomach clenched.

Liza smirked in the rearview. "What did you do to him, little Lulu? The boy has got it bad." She sounded impressed. But Lucy felt terrible.

It had been surprisingly easy to make Colin fall in love with her because Lucy naturally understood him—he was just like she used to be. That, plus the bit of illicit extra magic that Olivia had slipped to her in the middle of the night, meant his love still burned bright even after more than six weeks of trying to painlessly defuse it.

"What does it say, Gilly?" Liza asked.

"Colin wants to know how you're doing and if you're okay, because he hasn't heart back from you in a while. And he would still love to take you for that ice cream if you're up for it. Then he sent another one saying sorry he meant 'heard' back, not 'heart' back. And then he wrote 'haha' in all caps."

"Oh," said Lucy. She winced. She recognized that tone, that anxious-slightly-desperate-trying-to-sound-casual-but-not-feeling-casual-at-all tone. She couldn't count how many similar messages she'd sent Alex.

"You do realize you can't just hide until he stops loving you, right?" Liza said.

"I know," Lucy said. But the truth was, she'd been hoping exactly that.

"Well, of course she *could*," Olivia said. "But it would be kind of mean, wouldn't it? To let him dangle like that?"

"Yeah, set him free, Lulu," Liza said with a smirk.

This was the part of being a Heartbreaker that Lucy was in denial about, that she felt quite certain she would not be able to do: the actual heartbreaking.

Lucy swallowed hard. She imagined Colin's face, and the way he stared at her the last time she saw him the day before she became a Heartbreaker—he was full of such sweet unassuming, earnest love.

For a moment the car was silent, and Lucy wondered if she was the only one with a ball of guilt slowly growing in her belly. She was pretty sure she was.

The silence was only broken by the tinkly bell of Gil's phone ringing. "Gilly-bean," Olivia said. "Someone named Shay is calling you." She tossed the phone behind her into Gil's lap. Gil hit IGNORE.

"Who's Shay?" said Liza. "Is that the Scottish one?"

Gil shrugged and then grinned. "Oh, who can even keep track anymore?" And she laughed. The rest of them laughed right along with her.

A few minutes later they pulled up in front of a small blue house. The paint was peeling, and it looked like the lawn hadn't been mowed in a month. The front walkway was lined with flower bushes half-overgrown, half-dead.

Liza opened the car door. "I'll just be a minute."

"We'll come up with you," said Olivia.

"You don't need to do that." Liza shook her head. "Seriously."

"Look," Olivia said. "We're not letting you deal with it alone." And with that she got out of the car and shut the door behind her.

Liza took a breath and then turned to face Lucy. "My mom is really messed up," she said quickly. "So please ignore whatever batshit thing she says. I just need to make sure she is not facedown in a pool of her own vomit because her job called and she didn't make it in today." Lucy had never heard Liza like this before—she sounded kind of ashamed. And just the littlest bit scared.

Lucy nodded and looked down at her lap. Gil had already told her about Liza's mom—about how she was a Glass Heart, which meant that her heart broke all the time, and every time it broke, it shattered. But Liza pretty much never talked about her.

Liza opened the front door and they followed her inside the house. "Mom, I'm here," she called out.

There was no answer, just the sound of the TV. They walked slowly. "I brought my friends, so please do not be drunk and naked. Hello?"

"Lizzie?" There was a quiet muffled voice coming from the bedroom. Liza pushed through the door into a dimly lit room.

There was a chandelier hanging from the middle of the ceiling, five of its six bulbs burnt out. There was a stained white carpet and in the center of it a large four-poster bed covered in a tangle of twisted sheets and blankets. The floor was littered with crumpled tissues and empty Diet Coke cans.

Liza went to the window and pulled open the curtains.

"Damn, Mom," she said. Sunlight streamed in. Sitting on the bed was a woman in her mid-forties, wearing a pink-flowered silk robe, her hair pulled back into a sloppy bun, eyes ringed in red. Even in this state, she was gorgeous. She held a phone up and pointed to a photo of herself in a liquid gold dress, fully made-up, laughing, holding on to the arm of a rather ordinary-looking man.

"You'd think that I would have been the one to leave him," she said. "I mean, look at us." She sounded so, so tired. "Look at me and look at him. He was just . . . he was just this guy." Her voice cracked on "guy." "I begged him to stay, though." She looked up then. "I don't know why he didn't."

"All right, Mom," Liza said. She walked over to the bed and started straightening out the blankets and putting the fitted sheet back on the mattress with the manner of an impatient but efficient nurse. She picked up a prescription bottle off the floor, opened it, and held it over her palm. A single orange pill bounced out. "These were supposed to last you until the end of the month."

Liza's mom didn't say anything—she looked down like an ashamed child.

Liza put the bottle on the nightstand and then started collecting up the bits of crumpled tissues, the half-crushed cans.

"I just don't understand why he left, Lizzie. I thought he was *it* for me. I was so good this time."

"You were with him for a *week*. How could you have

thought it was going to be forever?" Liza faced her mother. They looked so much alike it was as though Liza was talking to herself in the future. Except, of course, Liza's future self would never be like this.

"I . . . ," her mother started. "Well, I guess it sounds silly now."

Liza's voice softened. "You were supposed to go to work today. Your boss called. You missed your shift."

"Oh, shit," and then Liza's mom froze. She stopped crying and raised her hand to her lips. "Can you call them and tell them I'm sick, sweetie?"

"No," Liza said. "They don't care. They said, 'If she's not dead, tell her she's fired.'"

"But what about our bills? Our rent is due next week. How are we going to pay it?"

Olivia reached out and squeezed Liza's shoulder. She whispered something in her ear. Liza shook her head. "Not again," she whispered back.

"It's nothing to me," Olivia whispered. "You know that."

And then they all stood there in silence for a moment.

"Hi, Kate," Gil said. Lucy turned. Gil was smiling sweetly. "Sorry you're having such a rough time of it."

"Gillian, honey," Liza's mom said. She blinked and looked around, then reached up and touched her hair as though she'd only just noticed there were other people in the room. "Oh, it's so nice to see you, doll!"

"Well, okay then." Liza clapped her hands together. "This has been buckets of fun. But I just came here to make sure you weren't lying here dead."

Liza's mom tried to laugh, but it came out wrong. "I'm okay, honey, really, I am. You are very sweet to come and check on me. I'm sorry about all of this. Can I make you girls a snack? I think we have some English muffins—I could make you some of those little pizzas you used to like. . . ."

Liza sighed. "No," she said. "We're on our way somewhere." She turned toward the door, and the rest of them walked out behind her. But at the last second Liza pushed past them, came back, and gave her mom a quick kiss on the top of the head. For a moment, there was a crack in Liza's gorgeous shiny exterior, and the heart inside, impenetrable or not, was suddenly visible in the expression on her face. But it only lasted a second.

"Let's go, girls," she said.

And just like that, it was gone.

Eight

♥

By the time they got to Olivia's house, everything was back to normal, or normal-ish anyway. The four girls got out of the car and made their way up the walkway. There was an envelope leaning against the front door, thick and midnight blue, sealed with crimson wax.

"Olivia, you got a very fancy-looking—" Lucy started to say.

"Holy shit!" Liza shouted. Liza dove for the envelope and held it to her chest. "It's here!!"

She ran inside. Olivia followed. Gil grabbed Lucy's arm and whispered in her ear. "This was what I was talking about.

This is what could save him." And before Lucy had time to respond, Gil went in after them.

A moment later they were all in Olivia's living room, curled up on the evergreen velvet couches, the dangling Moroccan lanterns all aglow, the large photograph of Olivia's grandmother Eleanor, who'd been a Heartbreaker before she died, staring down at them from above the fireplace.

"Ladies," Olivia said. "Behold." She held up the envelope and broke the wax seal. A puff of smoke escaped and swirled into the faces of four beautiful women, each with a finger raised to her lips. Then a gust of wind blew out of the envelope and whispered, "SSH," and the faces were gone.

Olivia took out a sheet of heavy midnight blue paper and unfolded it twice. It was a list of about fifty names, each next to an age and a job.

Without speaking, Olivia reached out and tapped the first one, EVAN AARONOVICH, 22, ENTREPRENEUR, and a puff of smoke swirled out and formed itself into the face of a guy with sleek feline features and a self-satisfied smirk.

Gil touched the next name, KYLE ANGEL, 19, COLLEGE STUDENT, and there appeared the face of an overgrown man-child with a devilish glint in his eye.

Olivia touched MAX ASHKIN, 20, FILMMAKER, who had a face like a hairy shark.

"What is this?" Lucy stared down at the list. Olivia tapped another name, and a face swirled up, an actor from a movie

Lucy had seen over the summer. JACOB JADE, 23, ACTOR.

"These are the year's Hard-Hearted Bastards," said Olivia. "Otherwise known as the HHBs."

"They've all done some really crappy things this year," said Gil. "In the realm of the heart."

"And now," Liza said with a grin, "it's payback time."

"What do you mean?" said Lucy.

"Every year the North American Sisterhood of Heartbreakers compiles a list," Gil said. "And gives it out to all complete Heartbreaker families. Then they host a contest called the Breakies. The first Heartbreaker family to break the heart of someone on this list wins."

"Wins what?"

Gil turned to Lucy and smiled meaningfully. "Wins *everything*."

"I've heard they're giving out a bottle of Diamonding Powder this year," Liza said. She rolled her eyes.

"What's Diamonding Powder?"

"It's basically the Holy Grail for Heartbreakers," said Olivia. "It's as versatile as a diamond, and as long-lasting. All of our spells and potions and things wear off eventually, but apparently anything you do with Diamonding Powder lasts forever."

"Nothing lasts forever," Liza snorted, then faced Lucy. "Some people say it was made by Queen Cleopatra and others say the Hope Diamond used to be bigger, and this was crafted from the extra missing carats. And there are a dozen other rumors about it, but they're all just that. Rumors. The powder isn't even real."

"Yeah, you're right," Gil said. She shook her head. "I mean, I've even heard that it can be used to give a regular person a heart as strong as a diamond." Gil turned to Lucy again. Their eyes met. "But I highly doubt a Heartbreaker would ever make a potion like that. What would be the point, right?" A tiny smile bloomed on Gil's lips. And Lucy felt a crazy rush of energy run right through her.

"*The Book of Love*," said Olivia. "That's the main prize, and that absolutely exists. And it's the most valuable thing of all. It contains everything the Heartbreakers know, all in one place. It's thousands of pages long and who knows how old. It's been secretly passed around for years. And in the last few it has been one of the prizes for the Breakies. The winning family gets to keep it for a year, before they have to pass it on."

"Didn't you say your granny had it once?" Gil said.

"She had this very big, very old book when I first moved in with her," Olivia said. "I asked what it was once and she wouldn't tell me. She just said not to touch it and then not long after it was gone."

"Well, you'll get to see it this year," Liza said. "When we win it." Liza fixed her eyes on Lucy. "The council has this rule that only full families of four are able to enter for the grand prize." She smirked. "So I guess it's good that you're one of us now."

"Why only full families?" Lucy asked.

"Every sister needs three others to keep her in check, and only complete families of four are considered strong enough to handle magic that powerful," Olivia said.

Lucy snuck a glance at Gil, who gave an almost imperceptible nod before turning away.

Olivia looked back down at the list and touched JACK CORNWALL, 26, FILTHY RICH. He had a face like a cabbage.

"Who's the lucky one . . . ?" Liza said, and she tapped her bottom lip with the tip of her finger. "Hmmm. Maybe?" She poked DEVON SHIRLY, 22, TECH BILLIONAIRE. Lucy remembered seeing an article about him online, about how he'd broken up with his longtime girlfriend as soon as his company went public, and used a bunch of his newfound cash to hire high-class call girls by the dozen. A face rose up—it looked awfully pleased with itself. "He'd be fun to break," Liza said.

"Possibly," said Olivia. "But think about how much magic we'd need to waste just to get access?"

"I read he's super paranoid and travels with three different bodyguards all the time," said Gil. "Although I guess considering this, maybe he's not so paranoid after all."

Lucy stared down at the list. She recognized some of the

names—the newly famous star of a recent blockbuster movie, rumored to have simultaneously dated three of his costars without any of them knowing; the heir to a billion-dollar cosmetics fortune; the son of a prominent celebrity lawyer.

"I don't know," said Olivia. "Maybe?"

"Eh," said Liza. "Not sure this would be any fun. He's not even cute."

"Wait," Gil said. "Wait, this is perfect." And she touched BEACON DREW, 18, ROCK STAR. And his face swirled up. Lucy instantly recognized it from the cover of his album, which was currently being advertised everywhere. He'd started out playing at underground blues and jazz clubs when he was only thirteen, but had only gained serious mainstream stardom when he started singing and playing other people's pop songs. He was known for being a huge "partier," and he was always popping up on gossip blogs with a never-ending stream of adoring hot women. Everything about him oozed complete utter jerk.

"Ah yes," Olivia said. "He'll do just fine."

Liza ran her fingers through her hair. "Well, hello there, stranger," she said to the remains of his face. Her breath blew the rest of him away. "He'll be a blast to break. I assume I'll be on offense?"

Olivia nodded. "Now we just need to figure out where to find him," she said. "Actually, wait, isn't he playing at a festival in a couple of days? Sound something?"

"SoundWave," Lucy said. "I think it starts this weekend. But tickets are impossible to get." Lucy only knew about it because Tristan was obsessed with going to it. He tried and failed every year because tickets always sold out within seconds.

"Impossible for *whom*?" Olivia said with a grin. "Well, so now that we have our target, it's time for a little research."

Olivia took a sleek laptop off the table and handed it to Liza, who started typing quickly.

A couple of minutes later Liza's mouth twisted into a smirk and flipped the computer around. On the screen it said, *WELCOME BEACON,* and there was what appeared to be his email inbox.

"What magic did you use to do that?" said Lucy.

"None." Liza shrugged. "I broke the heart of a hacker once, and he taught me a few things first."

Lucy read over Liza's shoulder. *TOUR DATES* was the first email subject. *I'M MAILING YOU MY PANTIES* was the second. They spent the next half hour combing his inbox for all emails to or from or about girls, but there were so many they eventually just searched for all emails containing the phrase "I love you." There were twenty-two from six different people. Three included naked pictures. "Too bad he's a dude and an idiot," Liza said. "He'd make a great Heartbreaker." She clicked through a few of the emails. "Hey, listen to this one he sent his manager. It's from two weeks after his last album came out. 'I don't want to be associated with this shit forever, it's barely even music.' Doesn't seem to think too highly of his own songs, apparently. Which shows he's not quite as stupid as he looks."

"Um . . . you guys?" Gil's voice was quiet. "There was something else in the envelope." She held up a sheet of what looked like shimmering cellophane. There was a broken heart printed on each of the four corners, and in the center was a golden thread twirling itself around and around. Gil put her thumb and forefinger over one of the hearts, Olivia pinched another, and Liza grabbed a third.

"Come on, apple pie," said Olivia, and Lucy reached out for the last one. As soon as she was holding the final heart, the thread started swirling itself into words.

Due to recent allegations that some families have been recruiting new sisters solely for the purpose of entering the Breakies, this year there will be an additional requirement for entry—not only must all families be complete with four members, but also each member must have broken at least one heart post–tattoo ceremony. The prizes in this year's pack are too powerful to be entrusted to new baby Heartbreakers. Good luck.

The thread swirled into a heart shape, then disappeared. Lucy looked down. She felt them all watching her.

"Lucy, this means . . . ," Gil started to say. But she didn't finish. She didn't have to.

If Lucy didn't break a heart, they couldn't enter the contest. And if they couldn't enter the contest, she couldn't save Tristan.

Lucy knew what she had to do.

Nine

Lucy woke to the sound of screaming. A second later, she realized the screams had been her own. The sky through her window was velvet black. The clock on her nightstand glowed 12:23. She reached her hand up and pressed her heart. It couldn't break, but it could still thump the hell out of itself. She'd been dreaming, she realized, dreaming about Tristan. In the dream, the two of them were on a boat, and the boat started to sink. Lucy could see the shore from where they were, and she remembered shouting, "We can swim! We're close enough to swim!" But Tristan just shook his head and opened a little door in his chest and took out his heart. He pressed a button on the side, and it started to inflate like a balloon. He handed it to her. "Use this," he said. And then before Lucy could stop him, he dove into the ocean and she knew it was too late to save him.

Half-asleep, Lucy reached for the phone. It wasn't until it had rung three times that she fully awoke, and quickly hung up. What was wrong with her? She didn't just call Tristan in the middle of the night no matter what time it was, knowing he'd either be up already or happy to be woken by her. She didn't call to tell him about a funny dream she'd just had, or to ask him to tell her a joke if she'd had a nightmare. She didn't call Tristan in the middle of the night anymore because she didn't call him at all.

Lucy lay back down. It was just a dream, she reminded herself. Tristan hadn't drowned. His heart was broken, but she was going to fix it. There was nothing to worry about now. She breathed deeply, trying to slow her heart.

A few minutes later, her phone began to vibrate.

HELP! AN EVIL WIZARD TRAPPED ME IN A PHONE! flashed on the screen.

Lucy stared at it for a split second, confused, and then smiled. Over the years, Tristan had programmed himself into her phone as dozens of different things. For a week last summer he'd been THE PRESIDENT OF THE UNITED STATES OF AMERICA and changed his ringtone to the national anthem. For another he'd been MY INTERNAL MONOLOGUE and would call and pretend to be speaking as Lucy. That past spring he'd been I'M STANDING RIGHT BEHIND YOU, and even though she knew it was him calling, she'd been incapable of seeing that flashing on her screen without turning around to check who was there.

Lucy raised the phone to her ear. "Hello?"

Instead of words she heard a *ssh*, a crackle, then music—a few bluesy harmonica notes, followed by an acoustic guitar and in the background the pat, pat, pat of drums. The music cut off and then Tristan began to speak. "Heeeey there, listeners." His voice was deep and low. "This is W-L-U-C-Y radio, broadcasting from Tristan's truck. You're live on the air."

Lucy smiled, her brain still thick with sleep. Her body flooded with relief. This was Tristan. Her best friend. Sounding exactly the same as he always had.

Lucy put on a fake nasal voice. "Longtime listener, first-time caller. Did I win the tickets?!"

Tristan laughed. And then there was silence.

"I hope I didn't wake you up," Lucy said. "I'm sorry for calling before, I just had . . ." She stopped. "I was just calling to say hi." Lucy bit her lip. "Were you sleeping?"

"Yes, I was sleep driving," Tristan said. "It's a good thing you called when you did."

"Sleep driving is very unsafe," Lucy said.

Silence again.

"Sorry I missed you before, bud, I was just saying good night to someone."

"Oh!" Lucy said. "Like a daaaaate?" She tried to sound teasing the way she might have before things got so weird between them.

"I don't know," Tristan said. "Nah. I don't think so. Maybe?"

And Lucy smiled because the response was so typical Tristan. "I don't go on dates," he'd told her once. "I hang out with people. And sometimes those hangouts include some smoochin'." He'd pronounced it just like that, without the G. As a joke. Except he wasn't kidding.

"Listen, are you at home?" Tristan went on, "I'm going to be driving right near your house in about three minutes. Think Suzanne and Georgie would mind if you pop outside and say hello to your buddy?"

Lucy hesitated only for a second. "Well, Suzanne and George can't mind if they don't know." She felt a wave of confused relief. Was she imagining or did Tristan sound happy? Like, *actually* happy. Was that possible? "I'll be outside in two," she said.

But before she left her room, she took out that tiny pot of almond-scented Empathy Cream and rubbed a dab into each palm. It felt wrong to look into Tristan's heart on purpose, but what choice did she have? If she wanted to help him, she'd have to break another heart. And if she was going to do *that*, she had to know Tristan needed her to, that there was just no other choice.

Ten

O kay," Tristan said. "Ready for the rest of it?" He leaned over and opened the passenger door, and Lucy slid in. He tapped the PLAY button on his phone, and the song that had been playing earlier kept going. The guitar stopped and was replaced by the rich and velvety notes of a cello. The harmonica came back in, and the sounds of the two instruments wrapped around each other, like two voices singing a duet. It was hauntingly beautiful right up until the very last note.

"My god," Lucy said slowly. "That was gorgeous. Who was that?"

Tristan shrugged. "Oh, go on, you sweet talker," he said. But when Lucy turned, she could have sworn she saw him blushing. "That was me and Phee."

"Phee?"

"She's who I was just with. She's a girl I met at the diner, and we got to talking about music and things. She plays cello and is a huge music nerd and has a whole studio thingy set up in her basement, so that's where we recorded this."

Lucy turned and looked at him. He brushed his hair off his forehead, a tiny secret smile playing on his lips. When their eyes met, she realized something:

The longing she thought she'd seen at the party just wasn't there. Instead, there was only that familiar twinkle of excitement. He looked like his old self.

Maybe his love for her hadn't been so serious after all. Maybe she was egotistical for ever having assumed it was. And whether it was or not, he now seemed to be over it.

They held each other's gaze, and Lucy felt a warming in her belly. It was funny, she'd been so scared of making eye contact with Tristan when she thought he loved her, that she'd barely seen him in quite a long time. "She's really talented," Lucy said.

"Freakily so," said Tristan.

Lucy smiled. "I'm really glad you came over."

"Me too." Tristan smiled back. "I missed you." He pulled

her toward him in a sudden hug. "Sorry I've been a little MIA lately."

Lucy felt the warmth of Tristan's body through his T-shirt. She felt herself begin to blush. It was just that they hadn't hugged in so long, that no one had really hugged her in so long except for maybe Gil. Lucy put her hand on his arm to steady herself. And then, just like that, Lucy couldn't move. She couldn't speak. She couldn't anything. Her hand was still on his arm. She closed her eyes. The blood drained from her cheeks. A drum beat in her ears.

"Luce? You okay?" Tristan asked.

But she wasn't. Not at all.

She felt a bolt of twisting pain in her heart, and a weight on her chest, so heavy it was hard to breathe. Underneath it all was a multilayered love that hit her in wave after wave, swelling so big she could have drowned in it.

Lucy looked down at her hand on Tristan's arm.

This was how Tristan felt—these were his feelings rushing through her.

It was worse than she could have possibly imagined. "Luce?" Tristan was staring at her, eyebrows knotted, like she was the one who needed worrying about.

Lucy pulled her hand away. His feelings drained out of her.

"Wow, you looked really freaked out for a second," he said. He tipped his head to the side.

"Yeah." Lucy tried to force out a laugh. "I don't know what happened there. . . ."

How was he going around in the world feeling like this? Getting up, going to school, meeting friends, going to parties? How was he even surviving?

The answer hit Lucy like a brick in the face: because Tristan was an expert at bearing pain and making it seem like nothing at all.

Tristan and Lucy became friends back in fourth grade, but she knew of him before that. Everyone did. He was the kid whose mom died. Her illness came on fast and he'd missed the last three months of second grade, then came back after the summer and done second grade again, all the while acting like nothing had even happened. Lucy remembered seeing him in the hall, noticing the way he smiled and joked with everyone. At the time Lucy decided he must not have loved his mother—either he was terribly mean or she was.

It was only two years later when they became friends that Lucy realized how wrong she'd been. He was the sweetest person in the world, and he'd loved his amazing mother endlessly. It wasn't that he'd actually been okay when he came back to school—it's just that he was a master of hiding his feelings, of burying them deep and putting on a smiling face. And since then, he had only gotten better at it.

"Lu?" Tristan said finally.

"I'm okay," Lucy said. "I'm okay. I'm just . . . suddenly not feeling that well. I think I should go back inside."

Lucy opened the door.

"Feel better, bud," Tristan said. And he smiled back, that same sweet smile as ever. But this time there was no chance of convincing herself she didn't know what was actually behind it. Or that there was any way around doing what she knew she had to do.

Eleven

YES!!!!!

Lucy stared at Colin's text and felt her stomach sink. Late the night before she'd sent him a message, asking if he was free that afternoon and wanting to do something. And she'd woken up to his response, sent at 6:01 a.m. Lucy squeezed her phone and shook her head. She imagined Colin smiling sweetly while he typed out his message, probably still cozy under the covers. She imagined him trying to decide how many exclamation points he should use and then deciding "Oh what the hell," and sending them all. She imagined him hopping out of bed, so happy and excited, because he had no idea what was coming for him, no idea that by the time he got back into bed, he'd have a broken heart. The whole thing made her sick.

But the alternative made her sicker.

Sometimes it isn't about choosing between right and wrong—it's about choosing between bad and worse.

When Lucy got to school, she desperately tried to ignore what was coming and just focus on the here and now. But it was impossible. There were eight hours left until she'd have to do it. What on earth was she going to say to him?

With seven hours to go, she saw Jason and Jessica in home-room, desks pulled up next to each other. They were staring down into their notebooks, but under their desks their fingers were intertwined. And Lucy found herself sending out a silent wish that neither of them would ever break the other one's heart.

T-minus six hours and forty-five minutes, Lucy saw Alex in photo class. He asked for her opinion on a photo he'd taken of the girl he'd cheated with, night swimming in a bikini. "Her ass is a bit overexposed," Lucy said, once again amazed that she ever dated someone so ridiculous. But was what he'd done to her any worse than what she was about to do?

Four hours went to three went to two went to one. And then the school day was done and there was nothing left to do but call the poor boy and get this over with. She hit TALK.

"Lucy!" Colin picked up after a single ring.

"Hey," Lucy said. She felt her throat starting to close, the words all stuck inside it. She couldn't continue, but she didn't have to because suddenly he was doing all the talking.

"I was so, so happy to hear from you this morning," he said. "I've been smiling all day. I was worried I'd scared you off by texting too much and seeming like a stalky weirdo—I'm usually really shy when it comes to girls. . . ." The words tumbled out in a jumble like he'd been rehearsing them. "The thing is, I just really like you, and I feel like we have some kind of weird special connection or something." He paused for a moment. "I know that sounds crazy, or really stupid." He continued more slowly. His voice was soft and low and when he wasn't rushing, actually kind of sexy. Too bad it was entirely wasted on her. Someone else would like him. Lots of other someones would like him. She just needed to set him free. "Especially since we don't even really know each other. I mean, for all I know, *you* could be the stalky weirdo. Ha! I'm just kidding. Sorry. I make weird jokes when I'm nervous, and I'm really nervous right now. I guess what I'm saying is, I . . ."

This was too much. Lucy had to stop him. "Listen," she said. "I feel like some ice cream. Do you want to take me out for ice cream?"

"I would absolutely love to," he said. He sounded thrilled. Lucy cringed. But she knew what she needed to do. And this time, nothing—not his sweet face, nor his kind eyes, nor the ball of guilt swirling in her stomach—was going to stop her.

Twelve

Thirty minutes later, Lucy sat watching Colin's back as he walked away. At the door he turned and gave her this sad little wave. Lucy waved back, then reached down for her tear-catcher necklace and squeezed. A tiny saltwater ocean was now trapped inside it.

Thank goodness this was over.

Thirty minutes before, he'd come bounding into Sundaes and Cones like a happy puppy and she still hadn't had any idea what she was going to say to him or how she was going to do it. He'd sat down in front of her all wide-eyed and smiley and "So did you see the video everyone's been posting . . . ?" and "Have you heard that new song . . . ?" as though he'd spent the entire afternoon coming up with conversation topics. And Lucy knew the time for careful planning had passed and she just needed to do it. The words were coming out of her mouth before she fully realized what was happening—"I'm sorry, Colin," she'd said, "I just can't do this. The you-and-me thing, I mean. I wish it didn't have to be like this. I'm really, really, really sorry."

She didn't even need Oscar Drops to make it sound sincere because what she said was true. She could not think of many times she'd been sorrier.

Colin was silent for a while after that. He looked down and then finally whispered, "Wow." A tiny tear quivered in the corner of his eye. "I was not expecting that," he said. He tried to smile and another tear collected.

Lucy said nothing. She felt a wave of embarrassment on his behalf, knowing it must be killing him to cry in front of her. But then she forced herself to take the final step—she reached out to brush that tear off his cheek. The Empathy Cream she'd smoothed into her palm confirmed the truth of his broken heart.

She quickly unscrewed her tear-catcher necklace and deposited the tiny droplet inside. She felt something then, in her chest, in her heart: an odd spreading coldness like she'd swallowed a too-big lump of ice cream, even though the sundae Colin had insisted on buying lay untouched between them. The coldness faded then, and a rush of energy went through her. She felt her mouth wanting to spread into a smile, and she had to consciously stop it from doing that. Colin looked up at her then.

"I just wish . . ." He stopped and chewed his lip.

And beneath the table Lucy was sticking her left hand in her purse. "What do you wish?"

He hesitated. Then shook his head.

"Make one," she said. "It might just come true."

And obedient boy that he was, he *had* made a wish. She saw it light up the star in her palm.

A few minutes after that, he stood and said he was leaving. He gave her a hug. His arms shook as he let her go.

Now Lucy sat alone, watching through the window as Colin walked across the parking lot. There was a group of junior boys sitting at the next table staring at her. She could feel their eyes on her skin. She turned and saw one of them lick his cone in a way Lucy could only imagine was supposed to be seductive.

Lucy ignored them. There was still one little thing left to do—she dropped the golden Wish Star on top of the sundae, scooped it up with her spoon, popped it into her mouth, and crunched down. She closed her eyes and then heard the sweet tones of Colin's voice as though he was whispering in her ear.

"Lucy seems so sad now," his voice said. "I just want her to be okay."

Lucy pressed her lips together. His own heart was freshly

broken, but that was what he'd wished for. She was, she realized, nothing like Colin. Not anymore, anyway. Breaking his heart had only been hard before she'd done it. And now that it was over, she barely felt anything at all.

He'd wished for her to be okay.

Well, lucky boy, it looked like his wish had already come true.

Thirteen

When Lucy got home, Olivia's blue convertible was parked out front with Lucy's three sisters sitting inside. As soon as they saw her, they started to clap, their applause growing louder and turning to cheers.

Olivia flipped on the stereo, sending loud dance music into the air. Liza shimmied her way out of the car. "Well, little bunny, you're a full-fledged Heartbreaker." Liza grabbed Lucy's hands and twirled her around. "Now you're *really* one of us."

Gil pulled Lucy in for a hug. "I promise it was worth it," she whispered.

"How did you guys know . . . ?" Lucy said slowly.

Gil smiled. "We're sisters. When one of us breaks a heart, we all gain power, and we all feel it in our own."

Olivia popped the trunk, then motioned for Lucy to come over. Inside was a pile of sleeping bags, duffels, and a tent. On top of it all was a black leather guitar case. Olivia lifted the lid, and Lucy stared at a guitar, dark wood inlaid with swirls of silver and gold. Lucy ran her hand over the smooth wood, then plucked a string. Even from inside the case she could tell it would sound amazing.

"That's yours," Olivia said.

"It is?"

"Think of it as a little congratulations present," Olivia said. "The first time is never easy."

"Oh my goodness. Thank you," Lucy said.

But Olivia just waved her hand. "Not that there's anything wrong with the guitar you had," Olivia said, her lips curving into a smirk. "But if you're going to be playing at the festival, you might want something a little prettier. . . ."

"What?" Lucy's head was spinning.

"You're playing at SoundWave," Liza said. "In the New Voices tent." She shrugged like it was nothing, but she was fully grinning now. "It's going to be a lot easier for me to get at Beacon if I meet him as a friend of a fellow performer rather than just some groupie. Not that I'd ever be *just some groupie*, but, y'know . . ."

"You're serious," Lucy said. "You're serious?"

Liza nodded. "You remember Paisley, our DJ friend? He set it up. He knows one of the bookers."

"It's not like you don't deserve it, though," Gil said. "He just played her the recording he made when you sang at Pete's that first time. And, of course, she loved it."

Lucy tried to let the meaning of their words sink in. But for some reason she couldn't really feel it. Why wasn't it sinking in? She pictured Colin's sweet sad face and quickly shut her eyes. She'd had no choice. It was over. There was no point in thinking about it anymore. She forced her eyes open and looked at the smiling faces of her sisters. "This is amazing," she said. "You guys are amazing."

"No, Luce, *you* are," Gil said quietly. "Thank you for doing what you needed to do, even though it was hard."

"All right," Liza said. "You're amazing, we're amazing, everyone's amazing. Put your ass in the seat—SoundWave awaits."

"Now? I need to go in and tell my mom I'll be gone. . . ." Lucy's head was spinning. "I forgot it was . . ."

"She's not home," Gil said. "But don't worry—I already took care of it."

"You did? Did you use . . . ?"

Gil laughed at Lucy's concerned expression. "No, I didn't do magic on your mother if that's what you're wondering.

She passed us on her way out, and I just told her we were going to stay at Olivia's house for the weekend because a boy dumped her and we needed to cheer her up. She said breakups are really hard and that we were very nice friends. She also said you should call her if you need anything."

"Okay," said Lucy. "Wow, great. I'll just run in and grab my stuff."

Olivia shook her head. "I think you might need some new stuff to go with that fancy new guitar of yours. We'll stop on the way."

And with that, Lucy hopped in, Gil shut the door, Olivia started the car, and Liza cranked the music. They drove off dancing.

Olivia was showing Bastian, the beautiful head stylist, a photo on her phone. "Something like this?" she said. "Maybe?" She swiped to another photo. "What do you think?" Bastian pursed his rosebud lips and furrowed his heavy brow. "Hmmm," he said. And then he steepled his fingers and closed his eyes like he was deep in meditation despite the pounding dance music.

It was two hours since they'd left Lucy's house, and this was their ninth stop in a whirlwind shopping extravaganza. They'd already gone to five different stores in a high-end mall, a shop selling handmade leather boots, an amazing vintage store, and a makeup outlet for makeup artists. At each new destination, Lucy barely had time to get her bearings before Olivia, Liza, and Gil marched up to the counter with a very careful selection of completely perfect items, all of which Olivia paid for with bills peeled from a large roll she kept in her tiny purse. The whole thing was kind of overwhelming.

And now there they were at some place called Cream, which looked like a hotel, sounded like a club, and was actually an incredibly expensive salon.

To Lucy's left, Olivia, Liza, and Gil sat themselves down in identical white leather salon chairs and started chatting with their stylists.

In the mirror, Lucy saw Bastian open his eyes, nod at himself, and then without a single word take a pair of gold scissors from the pocket of his black leather pants, and begin to snip.

An hour and a half later, four girls stood side by side in front of Cream's huge gilt-edged mirror. There was Liza, whose streaky mane was now a bit streakier; Gil, whose pixie cut was highlighted with chestnut; Olivia, whose roots had been touched up and whose hair was an inch or two shorter in length; and a mystery girl Lucy had never seen before—some badass rock chick who was apparently supposed to be Lucy.

Badass rock chick Lucy had bright blonde, almost white

hair, which had been teased and tousled and highlighted with the thinnest streaks of gold, actual shiny metallic gold as though strands of her hair had been dipped in something precious. She was wearing a charcoal-gray silk bra and a sheer white T-shirt printed with the logo of some obscure band Lucy had never heard of. Liza had borrowed a pair of hair-cutting scissors and chopped the top off, so the newly enormous neck hole kept drooping off the badass girl's shoulder. She was wearing so many bracelets on each arm, they looked like a cross between jewelry and glittering armor. On the bottom she had on a short dark denim skirt, and a pair of maroon ass-kicker boots. Her eyes were ringed in dark liner. This girl didn't just look ready to play a single song at a festival, she looked like she was ready to headline the whole damn show.

"Bastian, you are magic," Olivia said. And then she went up to the desk and paid the absurdly large bill.

The four girls headed back out into the parking lot.

"Well, sisters," Liza said, her voice a throaty purr, "I guess all that's left to do is go and break a heart."

The sky was the color of a ripe nectarine when they pulled into the SoundWave lot and Olivia popped the trunk.

A guy was sitting in the back of a truck with three friends watching them. "Welcome to the Wave, ladies," he said.

He was about their age and had a smooth Southern accent. "Need help carrying your stuff?"

Liza reached into the trunk and yanked out an enormous bag. "Nope," she said. "But let me know if you boys do."

Five minutes later, they were approaching Tent City, their temporary home for the duration of the festival. The big show didn't start until the next morning, but already the campgrounds were starting to look like a tornado blew through carrying a postapocalyptic carnival city, and left it there. There were tents everywhere, from little two-person pop tents to enormous canvas contraptions that could easily hold ten. A few people rolled their sleeping bags out right onto the grass. In the center of the field a girl and three guys were hammering the final spokes into a large teepee that stretched fifteen feet into the air. The outside was decorated with gold flowers that glittered in the orange glow of the setting sun. Off to the side, a girl was playing an accordion and another girl was playing a guitar, and they were singing. Lucy turned to get a better listen and spotted a Heartbreaker tattoo popping over the top of the guitar girl's tiny stripy strapless dress.

"Olivia," Lucy whispered. "Look! I think that girl is a . . ." Lucy knew that other Heartbreakers existed, of course. But she'd never seen one in person before. The girl had short dark hair, high cheekbones, and bright red lips. She was stunning.

Olivia just shrugged without turning. "Yeah, you'll see some of that here. I'm sure we're not the only ones who picked Beacon as a target."

"Don't look so worried, Lulu," said Liza, "they have nothing on us. Besides, if it was too easy"—she turned and grinned—"it wouldn't be nearly as much fun."

Fourteen

Within an hour the place was packed, but once Lucy got used to looking for other Heartbreakers, they were easy to spot. They had a glow around them, a shimmering golden sort-of-halo that Lucy remembered seeing that very first night, when through Olivia's window she watched Gil break Ethan's heart. Gil and Lucy wove their way through the crowd of cute music nerds, design geeks, hipsters, festival followers, and photo junkies taking pictures with their fancy giant-lensed cameras. Lucy spotted four girls with the glow to her right, laughing as they dipped their fingers into a tiny pot of what Lucy knew must be Empathy Cream. But none of that mattered now—Gil and Lucy were on a mission.

They passed through a high chain-link fence out onto the enormous field where the concert would officially begin in the morning. A half-dozen eighteen-wheeler trucks were parked on the grass. Dozens of people in SoundWave Crew shirts were busy unloading equipment. A hundred yards away the main stage rose up into the sky.

There was a very tall woman standing in the center of the field, black hair flopping down over her face, her head shaved on either side of the flop. She was holding a tablet computer and tapping at it in a way that implied she was very important, or at least very official.

Gil marched right up to her. "Hi," said Gil. She smiled brightly.

"What do you want?" The woman put her hand on her hip. The tips of her nails were painted red, as though she had been clawing at something bloody.

"We're here to see Vicky," Gil said.

"And you are?"

"I'm no one." Gil smiled. "But my friend is Lucy Wrenn."

"Is that supposed to mean something to me?" She gave Lucy a look. Lucy felt herself shrivel.

"She's singing tomorrow in the New Voices tent. We were told to come by and check in?"

"And who are you, her manager?" The woman snorted. "Well, the good news is that you don't have to look for Vicky anymore because you're standing right in front of her. The bad news is she has no idea who the hell you are or what the hell you're talking about. And Vicky doesn't make mistakes."

"Our mutual friend Paisley played you her tape and helped set this up."

"I don't have a friend named Paisley."

"Are you sure? DJ? Really hot?"

Vicky shook her head. And then snorted again. "DJ? What is this, 1998? You must be talking about Vicky, V-i-i-k-i is how she spells it, which should give you some sort of idea of the type of person she is."

"Well, can we see V-i-i-k-i Viiki, then?" said Gil.

"She's gone."

"Where is she?"

"She left."

"But she was supposed to put Lucy on the list of performers."

"Well, I don't know what to tell you—she didn't do lots of things she was supposed to do, hence my being here right now." The woman clenched her jaw. "The lineup is already full. And your friend isn't on it."

Gil smiled calmly. "She was only going to sing one song, though. So you could probably put her on the roster, right?" Out of the corner of her eye Lucy saw Gil grabbing something out of her little brown leather purse. Then Gil pretended to scratch her neck and as she did, slipped what looked like a glittering earplug into her ear.

"Yeah, I *could*," Vicky said. "But why would I?"

Gil paused for a moment. "I'm sure you were dealing with enough already, having to work with that girl in the first place. And now that she's gone, you're probably doing two full jobs. Sorry, that's a really crap situation. We'll leave." Gil linked her arm through Lucy's as if to go. Then she stopped and cocked her head. "Out of curiosity, where did she go? Run off with some guy or something?"

Vicky rolled her eyes. "Yeah, good guess. One of the guys in Monster Hands, actually. Last night." A frown flashed across her face. A moment later it turned into a scowl. "And she left me to clean up her mess, of course."

"From what Paisley said, she was always a star-chaser. Not even cool or hot or interesting, she just fawned over anyone famous. Pathetic." Gil shook her head. "I'm sure in a week they'll be back, her begging for her job and him wishing he'd never made such a dumb choice. Sucks that she left you so much to do, though."

Vicky nodded. "Yeah." She took a breath. "It kind of does." She paused. "What did you say your name was again?"

Gil smiled. "I'm Gil. And this is Lucy."

Vicky nodded again. "Listen, I shouldn't be doing this, but"—Vicky smiled a tiny little smile—"Viiki had added a couple of her friends to the list last minute when we had a few spots left to fill. How about we just say she forgot to tell me about one of them . . ." Vicky swiped her finger across the screen and drew up a list of names. She crossed one out. ". . . but remembered to tell me about you. What's your last name, girl?" Vicky looked at Lucy.

"Wrenn," said Lucy. "W-r-e-n-n."

Vicky typed it in. "Well, there we go," she said. "You're on tomorrow from four fifteen until four twenty-one. And you know what? What the hell, here." She reached into her pocket and fished out a couple of vinyl straps. "These are all-access bracelets. Put these on and show them at any of the restricted areas, like the backstage pavilion or the jam tent." She cocked her head toward a large white tent off behind the stage. "It's this corny idea the organizer had, supposed to foster collaboration or something." She waved her hand. "Anyway, wrists." Gil and Lucy stuck out their arms, and Vicky snapped the bands around them. "Technically these are only supposed to be for the 'big names,' but whatever. Most of them think they're too important to have to wear them."

"Thank you so much," Gil said. She leaned in and gave Vicky a hug.

"It's nothing," she said. But behind her grimace was a hint of a smile. "Just promise me you won't fall in love with any rock stars."

"Oh, trust me," said Gil. "That is the very last thing that would ever happen." Gil slipped her arm through Lucy's again. "Good luck with the guy, by the way. He doesn't deserve you."

Vicky stared wide-eyed as Gil led Lucy away.

"What was that about?" Lucy whispered. "What did you put in your ear?"

"A Listen Between the Lines Plug," Gil whispered back. "Turns down the volume on what doesn't matter, turns up what does. And it turns out our new buddy Vicky over there thought *she* was going to run off with the guy from Monster Hands and . . ." Gil stopped. "Lucy, *LOOK.*"

Without another word, Gil pulled Lucy toward the jam tent, and as they got closer, Lucy realized someone she recognized was standing outside. She'd last seen his face in a puff of smoke. And before that, in a million ads for his album. Standing right there, talking on the phone, was Beacon Drew. Gil pulled Lucy forward. Her stomach tightened.

"Shouldn't we go get Liza?"

Gil shook her head. "By the time she gets here, he could be gone. And she doesn't have a bracelet. Besides, look. . . ." Gil motioned to two girls approaching from fifty feet away, surrounded by the Heartbreaker glow. "Magic or no, when a moment presents itself, you grab it and you hang the hell on." Gil smiled, but there was something fierce in her eyes.

She started toward the tent again. Lucy followed. An enormous mountain of man stood in front of the tent flap, blocking their way.

"Bracelet, girly," said Mountain.

"Oh, sorry, of course." Gil pointed to hers and then moved like she was about to enter.

Lucy glanced to the side. Beacon was still on the phone.

"No," Mountain said. He held up his laser scanner like a gun. "I need to scan it." And he held up his scanner gun like he was getting ready to shoot. Gil glanced at Lucy and shrugged. She held out her wrist, and Mountain flashed a red line of light across the band.

Then he gazed in the back of the scanner and shook his head. "Well, I'm sorry, *Mr. Deruth*, but I believe you're already right over there enjoying our delicious selection of microbrews." He pulled back the curtain and pointed toward a short round man draped in gold chains, drinking a beer.

"Oh, oops," Gil said. "We must have gotten the wrong bracelets or something." She smiled.

Mountain leaned down and lowered his voice to a soft growl.

"Listen, groupie, if you belonged inside, I'd recognize you. I don't know how you got those," he said, "but it's time for you to move along."

"No, you don't understand." Gil smiled again. "My friend

is a performer. So I'm sure there is some mistake. . . ." As she spoke, Gil reached into her purse.

Mountain stood back up and crossed his arms. "The only mistake here is the mistake you're making in not getting out of my sight before I stop feeling so generous and get you kicked out of the damn festival."

Lucy felt herself blush and her heart began to pound. Beacon was off the phone now, and he was walking toward them. If Gil was going to do anything, she was going to have to do it damn fast because five . . . four . . . three . . . two . . .

"Gil," Lucy whispered.

But it was too late. There he was, Beacon Drew, beautiful and cocky in a brown leather jacket. "Hey, Steve." He patted Mountain on the back. "What's going on over here?"

"Just a couple of groupies trying to sneak in, Mr. Drew—don't worry, I've taken care of it."

"Groupies, you say." He grinned and rubbed his hands together. "I love me some groupies." He turned. "It's cool, I've got this, man." And with a final irritated glance at Lucy and Gil, Mountain Steve backed inside.

"So, groupies," Beacon said. He crossed his arms. "Who are you here to groupie for?"

"No one," Gil said. "Lucy's a singer. She's singing in the New Voices tent tomorrow."

"Oh, is she?" Beacon raised an eyebrow. "So . . ." He faced Lucy. "Sing something, then." It sounded like a challenge. He leaned back, waiting for her to begin.

"Right now?" said Lucy. Her voice cracked.

"Well, you could sing two minutes from now instead, but I won't still be standing here. . . ."

Lucy's throat was so tight. It was one thing to sing in front of a bunch of friends at Pete's. But this . . . this was an entirely different thing. She looked at Gil, who was nodding. Gil mouthed, *Go*. But Lucy couldn't make any sound come out.

"So is this supposed to be some kind of avant-garde silent singing thing?" Beacon smirked. "I don't know if the SoundWave crowd is evolved enough to appreciate it."

Out of the corner of her eye, Lucy saw Gil stick her hand in her bag again, and when she took it out, the tip of one finger was covered in red powder. She popped her finger in her mouth, took it back out, clean, and then she leaned in toward Lucy. Very quietly she hummed a few notes, then blew a stream of cinnamon-scented air between her pursed lips. Lucy felt it curling up her nose. "Sing, Lu," Gil said. And then, without thinking about it, Lucy opened her mouth and a song came out.

If you'd give me one chance
To show you my love, baby

It was some silly pop song that played constantly on the radio—they'd even heard it on the way there. The original version was fast and dance-y, made for being blasted at some cheesy club.

I'd give you a chance
To dance into my heart

But Lucy slowed it way down and amped up the rasp in her voice.

I said, dance, dance, dance right into my heaaaart

She closed her eyes and pretended she was somewhere else.

That's where you belong, girl.

She finished on a high note.

Beacon did a slow clap. "Pretty big balls you got there, kid." He smirked.

"Sorry?" said Lucy.

He raised an eyebrow. "Takes some rather mighty testicles, your singing that song to me. I'm impressed you fit them into that tiny skirt."

Lucy felt her face grow hot. She had obviously failed his coolness test with that stupid song. She hadn't even *meant* to sing it, really. It was like it had just wanted to come out of her mouth, and so it did. Lucy shook her head. "I don't know why I sang that. I think it was playing in the car on the way here or something." She stared down at her boots.

Gil was nodding. "Yeah, isn't that the song you said sounded like it was written by a crappy songwriting robot? Like it had no soul at all?"

Lucy stared at Gil. She actually hadn't said that, or anything like it. What was Gil doing? "Um," Lucy said. "Maybe?"

Gil looked Beacon right in the eye. "Oh, no, wait," she said, tipping her head to the side. "It was me who said that."

And all at once, Lucy realized something terrible: He hadn't called her ballsy because the song wasn't cool—he'd called her ballsy because *this was his song.*

"Is that right, girly?" Beacon wasn't looking at Lucy anymore. "That's a new one. Eight Track called it a 'horrible parasitic ear-worm that will possibly eat your brain.'"

"Aw," said Gil. She reached out and put her hand on Beacon's arm. "Well, I wouldn't go *that* far."

What was Gil doing? Lucy had to stop her!

"Gil," Lucy leaned in. "That's his . . ." But before Lucy could say anything else, Beacon opened his mouth and closed his eyes, and this great big laugh was rolling right out of him. For a moment, watching him laugh, Lucy understood exactly why it was that he was famous. It wasn't just his looks or his music, not really anyway. It's that there was something magical about him. It was different than Heartbreaker magic. But still somehow intoxicating. "When my manager first played it for me, I was like, 'Desmond, this is shit!!' But he somehow managed to convince me to record it anyway. According to my accountant, it paid for both the beach houses I bought this summer. Which makes it lucrative shit, I guess, but still shitty."

"Sorry," Gil said. Her eyes were twinkling.

Beacon shook his head. "Don't ever apologize for telling the truth. Even if you're the only person around that's doing it." He paused. "Hey, listen, what are you guys up to later? Because I'm having a little party at my trailer. Starts at midnight, so if you're not busy . . ." He was staring straight at Gil. "I could use a couple of truth tellers at this thing."

Gil smiled. "I think we could probably find time to swing by."

Fifteen

Tent City bloomed after the sun set. Bonfires rose up out of the ground like glowing desert flowers, and guitars and drums and portable speakers appeared from nowhere as if dropped from the sky. All around Lucy and her sisters, people were flirting, mingling, bumping into old friends, and making brand-new ones. A bicycle-powered blender was carried in, and a girl in a belted picnic dress and a skinny guy with a Mohawk took turns pedaling it to blend fruity spiked slushies. Gil made friends with the guy riding the slushie-cycle, who brought them round after round of brightly colored concoctions, most of which disappeared down Liza's throat. "Are you sure?" Gil said after her third.

"Want me to ask for a virgin one next time?"

"When have I ever wanted a virgin *anything*?" Liza said. Her voice sounded playful, but she shot Gil a hard look.

Time passed and the air got cooler. Lucy and her sisters moved off to the side. For a while it was just the four of them, wrapped up in fuzzy sweaters, sipping coffees now, people watching. Midnight was approaching, and the later it got, the harder it was for Lucy to sit still.

"Check them out." Liza motioned toward three girls teetering in tall heels and short dresses. One stumbled in the grass, and her two friends caught her by the elbows. "If you can't walk in them, you don't deserve to wear 'em," Liza said, her voice just a little too loud. One of the girls gave Liza the finger. Liza shrugged, then took her flask out of her boot and topped off her coffee.

"Liza," Olivia said. There was a warning in her voice. Liza pretended not to notice.

Lucy looked at her phone. It was 11:22. She stood up. "I'm going to find the bathroom," she said.

"Make sure you're back in half an hour," Liza said. "Because you can bet your ass we're not the only Heartbreakers who'll be there." She took another long sip of coffee and then upended her flask over the cup.

Lucy made her way forward in the dark. The truth was, she just needed to walk. In less than an hour they were going to see him again. And then they would find out if this was going to work . . . or wasn't.

Lucy started strolling, no real direction in mind. She passed a dark-haired guy in a blue plaid shirt who was watching her walk. When their eyes met, he gave her a shy smile. Lucy smiled back out of habit.

"Hey there," he said.

"Hi," she said. And she kept walking. She could feel him staring at her as she went.

Embarrassing as it was to remember, Lucy knew there was a time, back before she met Alex, when this tiny connection would have filled her belly with a sizzle of excitement and she would have spent the rest of her night thinking about that guy, wondering if she should have stopped. But now she felt nothing. She knew how easy it would be to go back if she wanted to. She could talk to him, flirt with him, and make him want her. Even make him love her, eventually. But what would be the point? Half the fun of flirting was the unpredictability, the fact that you didn't know if it was going to work out. Now she knew it always would. But at the same time, it never could. Not really.

Lucy took a deep breath and shook her head. Why was she even thinking like this?

There was music coming from somewhere nearby, something bluesy and rhythmic. She wanted to hear more. She wove her way between tents and lawn chairs, over bodies, until she found a small group sitting around a campfire, their faces lit by its warm glow. As she got closer, she could pick apart the individual threads making that fabric of sound—the guitars, the hands clapping, and the thunk of a drum, and above it all a familiar wail. The curving, bending notes of a harmonica played by someone who knew just what to do.

Lucy stood there outside the circle looking for the source of that wail.

And then she found it.

Tristan?

There he was, harmonica held to his lips, hands cupped over it, eyes half-closed. The other instruments dropped out one by one, and then it was just Tristan playing a blues riff while a long-haired girl hit a wide flat drum. All around the circle, people were bopping to the beat and cheering along. When Tristan and the girl finally finished, everyone broke into shouts and claps.

"Damn, kid," someone said. "You can really play that thing."

"Hey, thank you," said Tristan. "Your fingerpicking is pretty unreal."

The short-haired girl to Tristan's right whispered something in his ear, and he laughed, then stood up. "All right, I'm grabbing drinks," he said. "Anyone want?" And he pointed to the people in the circle. "Beer, lemonade, water, beer, beer, soda, and a marshmallow." One by one the heads nodded and Tristan started walking toward the big blue cooler right next to Lucy.

Lucy was struck with the odd feeling that what she needed to do was to turn, and to run, that he shouldn't see her there just now. But it was too late, because there he was standing right in front of her, taking in her new hair, her makeup, her outfit.

"Hey, lady." Tristan put his hands in the pocket of his dark red hoodie and grinned, mock casual. "Do you happen to have a cousin who goes to Van Buren, because you look a lot like someone I know."

"Hi!" she said. She felt suddenly embarrassed, like a kid playing dress-up or a poser who'd been caught by the one person she couldn't fool.

"You look like a whole other person!" Tristan said.

Lucy's face was getting hot. She pushed her hair out of her eyes. "I came with Olivia and them. And they decided to go shopping along the way, so . . ." Lucy exhaled. "Anyway, nice harmonica playing." She felt like she was talking to someone she'd just met. "Who are you here with? How did you get tickets?"

Tristan turned back to the circle. "Phee!" he called. The short-haired girl looked up. "C'mere for a second?" She stood and started making her way over. The long-haired girl with the drum was watching them.

"Phee, this is Lucy," Tristan said. "Lucy, this is Phee." Phee was small and wiry, with dark hair and olive skin. When she smiled, dimples appeared in both cheeks.

"I've heard a million things about you," Phee said.

"Don't worry," Tristan said in a mock whisper. "I didn't tell her about the jewel heist or the secret meth lab."

Phee laughed.

Tristan continued, "Phee's a musician too. An amazing cello player. You heard her in that song I played for you the other day."

Lucy closed her eyes. She could still practically feel that music in her belly. "That was really beautiful," she said.

"*Pssssh.*" Phee shook her head. "Thank you, that's nice of you to say, but"—she turned to Tristan—"you weren't supposed to play that for anyone, bud." Phee punched him in the shoulder. Then she turned back to Lucy. "I'm an okay cello player. Tristan is very generous."

"I'm not generous at all!" Tristan said.

"Well, not when it comes to pancakes, you're not." And they both laughed.

Lucy forced a smile. Her face felt like plastic.

"And she's a big ol' dork too," Tristan said. "You know how I've been trying to get tickets for years but never could, because it's pretty much impossible?" He turned to Phee. "Tell her how you got the tickets." Then he turned back to Lucy. "This is nuts."

"It wasn't a big deal. I found out that the ticket sale section of the site actually goes live six seconds before it shows up on the page, so I wrote a little program that would grab tickets as soon as they were technically available and then ran it on three computers so there was no chance of my missing them."

"She is a crazy genius." Tristan nodded.

Phee shook her head. "It's just one of those things that sounds way harder to do than it actually was." She looked back up at Lucy. "So, Tristan told me you're a singer? We're just playing around over here—want to sit in with us?" Phee motioned to the fire, to the half dozen people around it. The girl with the long dark hair and the flat drum was watching them still, staring at Lucy so intently. And then Lucy realized why—the girl had a mark on her chest. A tattoo. Right over her heart.

"Did you come here with all these people?" Lucy asked.

"Nah, they just heard Trist playing harmonica while we were walking by and invited us to trade music for marshmallows. They're homemade ones from a sweet shop where some of them work. And they are *amazing*." She slung one arm around Tristan's shoulder, then held her other hand up next to her mouth and whispered loudly, "He uses me for my tickets, and I use him for his access to treats."

"This girl may be an even bigger sugar fiend than I am," Tristan said.

Lucy forced a smile, but her stomach twisted.

The Heartbreaker girl was still watching. She caught Lucy's eye and smiled a funny little smile. It made Lucy uneasy. All of this was making Lucy uneasy.

"I should probably get back . . ." Lucy said.

Someone threw another log on the fire, and the flame flared brighter.

"Well, if you're around tomorrow, we'll be at the New Voices—" Phee started to say.

"What time is the guy you wanted to hear on at?" Tristan said.

Phee took a phone out of her pocket. "They just updated the lineup. . . ." She poked at her screen. "Red Rover are playing at four, and I definitely want to see them, and then Jamie & Jamie are right after, and then Karl Black and . . ." Phee looked up. "Wait. Isn't your last name Wrenn?" She turned toward Tristan. "Did you say her last name was Wrenn or am I completely making that up?"

Lucy bit her lip. She realized what was happening, and there was no way to stop it.

"Well, if you're making it up, then you're psychic," said Tristan.

Phee looked at Lucy, blinking and shaking her head. Then she pointed to her phone. "Wait . . . so that makes you Lucy Wrenn. Are you . . . ?"

Lucy felt herself blushing again. She nodded.

"Dude, why didn't you tell me your friend was playing in the New Voices tent?" said Phee. "That's completely amazing!"

Tristan smiled. "Well, because I didn't know." But he

didn't look hurt that she hadn't told him, not like when she'd performed at Pete's house. Now he just looked happy for her. "That's incredible, Luce."

"A friend is friends with one of the bookers, so . . ." Lucy wished they would stop staring at her. "It's not really anything."

The Heartbreaker was still watching her too.

"Not anything?" Phee was shaking her head. "It is a huge deal!" She turned to Tristan. "We should get there early to make sure we can get up front for that."

"No, you guys don't have to, it's . . ." Lucy wanted to say she hadn't really earned it. That she hadn't earned any of it. But instead she just said, "I'm only playing one song—it'll be over so fast, you guys really don't have to come . . ." She looked at Tristan and Phee, standing there together—his eyes were glowing in the light of the fire. "I guess I should head back to . . ." She pointed behind her. "I'll see you guys later, okay?"

And when Lucy's eyes met Tristan's, she tried to somehow tell him everything with her gaze, to explain what she was trying to do, that she was doing this for him. But there was no understanding there. No, of course there wasn't. Phee poked Tristan in the side and he grabbed her hand. And the two of them started thumb wrestling. "You're mine, thumby," Phee said, laughing.

Lucy looked up one last time. She locked eyes with the

Heartbreaker. The girl winked. Lucy's heart was pounding when she turned to go.

She walked through the crowd again, back toward their tent. Up in the sky there was a tiny trail of light as a falling star dropped down to the horizon. She stopped then. And she closed her eyes, ready to make a wish like she always did, like she'd always done ever since she was a kid. But in that moment she wasn't even sure what she was supposed to wish for.

Sixteen

From fifty feet away, it was obvious the party had already started. Beacon's trailer sat in the middle of the field, silver and sleek, glowing from within. Thirty or so guests were milling around outside it, sipping drinks, flirting, dancing. Dotting the lawn were a half dozen picnic tables. Tiny fairy lights were strung up between the trees. The crowd was moving slowly, orbiting around someone. And who was in the center? Beacon, of course. There he was, sitting at one of the picnic tables facing out, watching the crowd. A Heartbreaker girl sat on either side of him, radiating a soft glow only Lucy and her sisters could see. One threw her head back in a fake-looking laugh and put her hand on his shoulder.

"Amateur," Liza said with a snort, and she smoothed her jeans over her hips.

They had changed into the new clothes they'd bought on the way—dark denim, corset tops, feather earrings, leather boots, stacks of bracelets. "Subtle rock chick with a hint of burlesque" was what Olivia had called the look. "Sexy and noticeable, but not over-the-top."

Liza licked her lips. "Ready or not," she whispered. "Here she comes." She started walking toward Beacon, swaying a little in her ankle boots. Olivia, Gil, and Lucy followed.

". . . so I just told him, 'Look, if you're not up for some serious hard-core debauchery, then you probably shouldn't even come on the tour, because when we party, we *party*.'" Beacon shrugged. "And he just couldn't handle it."

One of the Heartbreakers laughed. "That is sooo sad," she said. "It's just like, *heartbreaking*, when people try to compete so far out of their league." The girl caught Lucy's eye. She smiled meanly.

"I know," Liza said back loudly. "People shouldn't bother trying if they know they're going to *lose*." But Beacon didn't even look up, and the Heartbreakers just rolled their eyes.

Liza grabbed Lucy's hand and pulled her closer to the table.

"Go say something," she whispered. Her breath smelled sharp.

"I . . ." Lucy hesitated. This was it. She took a tiny step forward. "Hi, Beacon," she said. Beacon either did not hear her or didn't care.

Lucy heard Liza snort. "Awesome," she whispered. "You're a conversational genius." Her whisper was too loud.

Lucy's heart was hammering. "Hi, Beacon," Lucy said again.

Beacon glanced at her. "What's up, ladies." He nodded and half smiled. He seemed different from when they had met him earlier. Before he'd had his own kind of magic glow. Now he was just the jerk on the album cover.

"This is pathetic," Liza said. She turned, took two steps, and stopped so close to Beacon it looked like she was about to try to sit on his lap. "So this is your party, right?" She put her hand on her waist. Beacon looked up and nodded.

"Well, where the hell do I get a drink?"

Beacon motioned toward the dozen or so coolers on the grass a few feet away, then turned toward the other Heartbreakers and shrugged. Liza sauntered over and pulled out a can of beer, popped the top, and raised it to her lips. When she turned back, he wasn't looking at her anymore. "To your shitty songs," she shouted, then took a long swallow.

The other Heartbreakers exchanged a look. Beacon just

blinked blankly and then put his hand on the lower back of the second Heartbreaker.

"All right," Olivia said under her breath. "That's probably enough of this." She walked forward, slipped one arm around Liza's waist, whispered something in her ear, and led her away. Gil, who had been quietly watching from afar, was suddenly standing next to Lucy.

"Liza gets like this when she's wasted," Gil said. "She's been on a mission since she got here. Drank like half a bottle of some guy's wine while you were gone earlier too." She shook her head. "And something tells me that the drunk-party-girl act isn't Beacon's favorite."

"No?" Lucy tipped her head to the side. "But what about that whole 'When we party, we *party*' thing?"

"Luce, have you seen him take an actual sip of his drink since we got here? Look, he's using his bottle like a prop but not actually drinking it."

Lucy watched as Beacon gestured with his bottle. The girls next to him took swigs of their drinks and he put his bottle down on the table. "My hunch is Beacon isn't nearly so hard-core as he pretends to be. Or as cocky. But let's just double-check on that."

Gil pulled Lucy off to the side. When they were far enough away, she reached into her bag and took out a little glass bottle with an eyedropper top. She dripped a drop in each of her eyes, handed the bottle to Lucy, and motioned for her to do the same. The drops felt cold, and for a moment the world was a big blur. When it came back into focus, everything looked different. A gorgeous-looking girl's features were now distorted and grotesque, a big muscle-bound guy's muscles had grown to twice their size. A tall guy was suddenly very short, and a short guy was suddenly very tall. Three thin girls had each gained about thirty pounds. Liza looked like herself but a more exaggerated version—bigger mouth, bigger boobs, smaller waist. Only Olivia looked exactly the same as she always had.

"I-drops," Gil whispered. "Lets you see people the way they see themselves." Lucy turned to Gil. She looked different too: flat and dull, plain and forgettable. Kind of how Lucy used to feel before she met the Heartbreakers.

"Check out our boy." Gil pointed at Beacon. Gone was the handsome guy with the cocky smirk, and in his place was a regular-looking kid with big ears and a goofy smile. "Huh," Gil said. "So here's my take: He still sees himself as this dorky music nerd. He appreciates when people criticize his songs because the actual music is what he really cares about. He feels like he doesn't really belong here in this 'cool' world, so he works extra hard at his persona. He believes that if anyone saw the real him, they wouldn't like him. He thinks he wants everyone to buy his bullshit, but my guess is that what he really wants is what everyone who spends most of their life faking it wants—someone who can see through the act."

Lucy turned toward Beacon. He was morphing back into his old self. Thirty seconds later, everyone was back to normal.

"You're really good at this," Lucy said.

Gil shrugged. "If you can't be the hottest, be the smartest." Her face clouded for a second. Then she smiled. "So anyway, I think we may need to help our sister out."

They made their way back to the picnic tables, where Beacon had Heartbreakers on either side of him.

"Hey, buddy," Gil said. "Your groupies are here." She grinned.

Beacon turned at the sound of her voice and smiled. "I remember you," he said. He stood up and started walking toward her.

"Beaks," one of the Heartbreakers called out. "Where are you going? It's time to do shots!"

"Just a minute," he said. But he didn't look back.

"I remember you too," Gil said. Then she lowered her voice so that only Beacon and Lucy could hear. "Only last time you weren't trying quite so hard." There was such warmth in the tone of Gil's voice, in the expression on her face, that her comment didn't come out mean the way it could have. "Must be exhausting."

Beacon seemed taken aback for a moment, then quickly recovered. "Yeah, I'm exhausted," he said. "Come to bed with me and we can sleep it off." He gave what was probably supposed to be a lascivious smile. It looked forced.

Gil just shook her head. "See? All that stuff you're doing there, you don't have to do that with me. All I'm trying to say is I think you deserve to relax every so often. And I get the feeling you're a guy who doesn't get to do very much of that."

"And you don't think this is relaxing for me?" He motioned to his party.

"Was that supposed to sound rhetorical?" Gil let out a little laugh.

"Yeah, that came out, um . . ." He looked down. "Wrong." When he looked up, his expression had changed ever so slightly. He wasn't the guy on the album cover anymore. "But if kicking back with a bunch of hot girls isn't relaxing, then I'm not really sure what is." He reached up and scratched the back of his neck.

"You know what I think?" Gil said.

"What's that?"

"I think you know *exactly* what you'd find relaxing. And it has a lot more to do with listening to some old blues records by yourself in your trailer than it does pretending to drink with a bunch of strangers. Am I close?"

Beacon tipped his head to the side, like he couldn't quite figure out what was going on. "Really close, yeah," Beacon said quietly. "Except it would be nicer not to do it alone."

Gil smiled. "You have any Little Walter?"

Beacon nodded, his look of confusion slowly turning to one of delight. "It's funny you mention that, actually. I just got a whole bunch of vintage vinyl online. Had it shipped here because I was so excited for it."

"Do you have his—"

"Stop right there." Beacon grinned. "Whatever you're going to ask about, I can already tell you the answer is yes. Because I have everything he ever recorded." He paused. "Um, we could go listen to some in my trailer right now if you wanted."

"Yeah," said Gil. "That sounds like a really good idea." And she nodded. "Lucy, do you want to come?" Gil turned toward her. Asking this was part of the act. Lucy knew what her answer was supposed to be.

"No, thanks," Lucy said. "I think I'll stay out here. Have fun."

Gil leaned in and gave Lucy a hug.

"How did you know about the records?" Lucy whispered.

"Liza isn't the only one who can hack into an email account," Gil whispered back. "Or an eBay account, for that matter." She kissed Lucy on the cheek. "See you tomorrow."

And then she turned to Beacon and took his arm. "Lead the way," she said.

"I promise I'll take good care of your friend," Beacon called to Lucy.

Lucy watched them walk away, arm in arm. *But it's not her I'm worried about,* Lucy thought. And for a single confusing second, Lucy felt sad. She knew that what was happening was a good thing—it was what they'd all wanted. But she could not help feeling suddenly kind of sorry for Beacon for the great distance between what he thought he was walking toward and what was actually ahead of him.

When Lucy finally turned, Olivia, Liza, the two other Heartbreakers, and pretty much everyone at the entire party were watching as Gil and Beacon made their way toward his trailer. He held the door for her and motioned *after you.* Right before she stepped inside, Gil turned back and for just a second she looked entirely like someone else. She winked at Lucy. Beacon followed her in. And then the door swung shut.

The three girls made their way across the field and back through the fence.

Lucy felt an odd hollowness in her chest, almost as though she was homesick, although she wasn't sure what or who or where she was homesick for.

"I could have done it, you know," Liza said. She was starting to sober up now. Maybe finally beginning to understand what had just happened.

Olivia didn't turn her head. She shrugged ever so slightly. "I think Gil has it covered now."

Seventeen

ucy lay there, breathing in the canvas-scented air, eyes
closed but so far from sleep. When the three of them
had arrived back at Tent City an hour before, Lucy had
expected Liza to declare that the night wasn't over yet—to
suggest finding guys, more drinks, a better party. Instead she
had simply stripped to her underwear and bra right there in
the field, climbed through the door of the tent, curled up in
a sleeping bag, and started to snore. Olivia had followed and
a few minutes later, she was sleeping too. And now there was
Lucy, dressed in a pair of pajama pants and a T-shirt, cheek
pressed against someone's balled-up sweatshirt. She'd been
trying to will herself to sleep, but every time she closed her

eyes, she saw flashes of images she wasn't sure she wanted to see—Colin's face as he walked away, Liza's mother on the bed, her own mother sitting in that chair in the living room, Beacon's hopeful smile, Tristan's expression when she broke his heart, Tristan and Phee laughing.

Lucy tried to focus on other things, to force the images out. What was Gil doing at that very moment? But it was impossible for her to imagine. The Gil in the trailer with Beacon was not a Gil Lucy had ever met before.

There were sounds coming from outside the tent—the patter of footsteps in the grass, quiet words, hushed laughter.

Lucy pulled herself out of the sleeping bag and shoved her feet into a pair of flip-flops, and then she reached up, unzipped the tent, and crawled through.

Outside, a dozen people were sitting on blankets, cuddled up together like kids at a sleepover party, watching one of the giant movie screens. Lucy stood off to the side. The film projected onto the screen was in a language she did not recognize, and she could barely read the dusty yellow subtitles.

Off in the distance, tents were lighting up and going dark like big fireflies sending secret messages.

The movie watchers laughed in unison.

It was cold out now, and Lucy pulled the sweatshirt more tightly around her. She wished she had her bike with her and could ride off somewhere, or even just around and around. Her muscles itched. She needed to move. She started to walk, weaving her way between tents and sleeping bags. She went slowly at first, then faster and faster until her legs burned and her heart pumped hard. And when the images tried to invade her brain, she walked so fast she left them behind her.

Boom.

Lucy didn't know how long she'd been out walking when the fireworks started.

Boom.

Lucy's heart lurched as light streaked across the sky.

Boom, boom, boom. Pink showered down. Orange and green sea creatures spread out their legs. Then the embers faded to their ghosts in smoke.

People were coming out of their tents now, flipping on flashlights as the sky lit up gold.

And there was Lucy, leaning back against the fence at the far edge of the field, watching it all. She was alone. And then someone was next to her.

"No matter how many times you see them," a girl's voice said, "they're never any less magical."

Lucy turned. Purple lit up the sky and the face of the long-haired Heartbreaker from the bonfire.

"Hey," said the girl. "I think we met earlier, right?"

Lucy nodded as yellow exploded overhead. "So I guess you guys are also here for Beacon," she said. There was no reason not to talk about it now, she supposed. Not since

Gil was already with him.

"Sure, but everyone else too. This whole thing, actually." A swirl of rainbow sparks shot through the sky. "You sure as hell don't get shows like this in Bridgewater." The girl shook her head. She grinned as the fireworks lit up her face again. She brought her hands up, cupped her mouth, and let out a *woo* of sheer wonder and pure delight.

How strange this other Heartbreaker was, how unlike Liza or Olivia, or even Gil now.

Lucy could make out the silhouettes of dozens of people standing outside their tents, heads back, arms pointed up toward the sky. Out in Tent City someone *woo*-ed back, then someone else, their joyous cries echoing through the crowd. The girl cheered one more time. And Lucy felt an odd surge of jealousy toward this girl, toward all of them.

"Your tattoo," Lucy said. "How . . ." She wanted to ask this girl how she was a Heartbreaker but could still somehow be connected to all of these people.

There was another flash of light, a swirl of pink and red and crimson. Only when Lucy turned toward the girl and looked again, she realized the mark over the girl's heart wasn't a locked Heartbreaker heart at all. The tattoo was a purple flower, with heart-shaped petals opened wide, vines and leaves curling underneath. She was just a regular girl after all, and yet there was something about her. . . .

"What about it?" said the girl.

"It's pretty," said Lucy.

"Thank you."

"Does it mean something?" said Lucy.

The girl smiled. "More than you could ever imagine."

And they stood there together until the fireworks ended, but neither of them said anything after that.

Eighteen

The first thing Lucy saw when she woke up was the empty spot in the tent where Gil wasn't. And the second thing she saw was the blinking light on her phone. She had a text from Gil: a little winky face all on its own.

"Did you guys get . . . ?" Lucy started to say.

Olivia and Liza were already awake. Liza was still in her sleeping bag, facedown in her pillow, letting out periodic miserable groans. Olivia was sitting cross-legged, finger-combing her hair.

"We saw," said Liza, her voice muffled. "We got it too."

"It's good news," Olivia said simply. "I can't imagine it

will be long before she's done."

"So what do we do now?" said Lucy. She sat up. Her head hurt and her mouth was dry. It was morning, only a few hours after Lucy had gone to bed, but somehow she was wide-awake.

"Nothing," Olivia said. She reached for a pair of dark jeans and a charcoal gray sweater. "We just enjoy the day. Your show is in a few hours."

Somehow with everything else going on, Lucy had barely even thought about it.

"Are you still doing that?" Liza said, rolling over.

"I don't know . . . ," Lucy said slowly.

"Well, what would be the point?" Liza sat up. There were pillow creases on her face and dried drool crust in the corners of her mouth. She was stunning as ever. "Gil's already with Beacon."

Olivia pulled her hair up into a bun. "But, of course, you could," Olivia said. "If you wanted to. Do you?"

Olivia turned toward Lucy. A show at SoundWave—did Lucy want to perform?

How strange that Lucy didn't really know, or care about, the answer.

An hour later, they stood out in the field with the food trucks, sipping coffees with two Heartbreakers Liza and Olivia knew.

"So that's it," Liza finished. "She's still with him. And I

think we can pretty much guess where all this is going."

One of the Heartbreakers shrugged. "That's nice, I suppose."

Liza smirked and turned to Lucy. "They're pretending they don't care that we're winning."

The other Heartbreaker rolled her eyes. "We're just here for fun," she said. "What could anyone give us that we don't already have?"

"Oh, I don't know," Liza said. She tossed her coffee cup toward a big metal trash can. It swooped right in. "Victory?"

"Oh, right," said the first Heartbreaker. "That." And they all laughed.

Back in Tent City, Lucy wandered. The bands had started playing a couple of hours before, and most everyone was off watching them. But there was Lucy, alone with her camera looking for something to photograph.

When she'd first started taking pictures the summer before, something funny had happened—she started seeing the world ever-so-slightly differently whether her eye was behind a lens or not. It was like she was always on high alert, and without even consciously thinking about it, she was constantly finding things that would give her that *ping*-y feeling in her gut, a feeling that could only be relieved by the click of a shutter.

Only now she could barely remember the last time she'd

really *needed* to take a picture. She wanted to feel that again, that sense of urgency, that deep inner itch. But as she walked through Tent City, all she saw were blandly pretty things—a bird in the air, a pile of flowers. She looked inside for the *ping*, for the pull, but there was just nothing there.

The New Voices stage was set under a miniature circus tent of red and white stripes.

Lucy stood down the stairs to the side, hair teased, rock chick outfit on, squeezing the neck of her brand-new guitar. Why was she doing this again? Why was she bothering? Even she wasn't entirely sure. Maybe she just needed to prove to herself she could do it—she could still feel that rush of connection she used to feel when she sang. Then again, maybe she was just bored. And had already put on all that eyeliner . . .

Up onstage a guy was whistling and playing a small set of drums. It didn't sound like much to Lucy, but when he finished, the crowd gave the closest thing to a standing ovation you could get from a bunch of people who were already standing. They must be an easy audience, Lucy decided. Which was good, because she was finally starting to get nervous. And it was her turn to go.

Lucy climbed the stairs and walked out onstage. She could feel a couple hundred people staring up at her. She unfocused her eyes a bit so she wouldn't have to see them.

"Hello," she said into the microphone. "My name's Lucy, and this is a song I wrote for . . ." She paused. She'd written it for Alex, but it was her song now. "Someone I cared about a lot, back when I was really stupid." She heard a few people laugh. She inhaled one last time, then opened her mouth and let out a note, high and clear.

Ooooooooooo
I see you here when you're not
I . . .

Lucy felt a sudden coldness deep in her chest, like someone had thrust her heart into a freezer. She took a breath as the coldness spread out through her torso, down her arms, to the tips of her fingers, carrying with it a buzzing energy. What was happening? She couldn't think about that now. She'd only sung one line. And the crowd would be expecting a next one.

I feel you here when you're not
I see your face in the sky when you're not here

She cringed as she heard herself.

You're always here, you're always here
You are you are you are

How had she ever written such corny lyrics? And sang them like she really meant them? And how had a crowd ever loved it?

She looked out into the audience. *Well, this one certainly didn't.* They looked bored. A girl whispered something to her friend. A guy was staring down at his phone. A couple linked arms and strolled away.

Lucy tried to ignore the crowd, to look away. But it didn't matter because she could imagine what they were thinking—here was just another girl with a kind of pretty voice singing about nothing that meant anything. Not to them and certainly not to her. She couldn't understand how it ever had.

She raced through the rest of the song, and finally it was over. There was a smattering of polite claps, and on top of them the sound of two people cheering like crazy. Lucy looked down at the crowd again, and there right up at the front were Tristan and Phee screaming their heads off. Olivia and Liza were nowhere in sight. Lucy left the stage.

Back on the ground Phee flung herself at Lucy and squeezed her tight.

"That was amazing!" Phee said. And Lucy thought for a moment what a kind person this girl must be to say that, to try to make Lucy believe it. Behind her Tristan was nodding. He held his hand out for a high five.

"Yeah, bud," he said. "That was really great!" But Lucy

could see from the look in his eyes that he didn't really mean it.

"Well," said Lucy. "At least that's over." And she forced a smile.

Up onstage, the next act had started. The crowd was clapping and stomping, Lucy's crap performance entirely forgotten as though it never happened at all.

Phee reached into her pocket and took out her phone. She stared down at the screen. "I just got an alert from the SoundWave boards." She began to read. "'With great apologies to his fans, Beacon Drew has pulled out of the concert, citing personal reasons and dehydration.'"

"Personal reasons *and* dehydration," Tristan said. "Hmmm."

"According to the world of internet tabloids, I believe that is always code for something else," Phee said. "Probably went on too big a bender last night."

Lucy pressed her hand to her chest, where she could still feel the last bit of coldness lodged in her heart. And with a sudden fierce clarity she realized exactly what had happened.

They'd won.

Nineteen

The drive back was a celebration, a traveling party in a baby blue convertible. Liza rode shotgun, flashing every other trucker that passed. Olivia sang along with the radio, loud and off-key. Gil just could not stop bouncing, bouncing, bouncing in her seat.

One of Beacon's songs came on, and Olivia cranked it up.

If you'd give me one chance
To show you my love, baby

Gil danced in the seat next to her and sang at Lucy. *My heaaaaart.* She held her hands up to her chest and mimed a heart beating in time to the music. Then she mimed breaking it. When the chorus came on, Gil shimmied her shoulders. She leaned in like Lucy was supposed to join her. Lucy did her best to fake it.

In a way she understood Liza's and Olivia's excitement—they'd entered a contest together, and they'd won. But somehow it struck Lucy as strange for Gil to be celebrating like this, and maybe a little bit wrong considering everything else. And Lucy could not tell if she was being fair or not.

An hour into the ride, they were waiting at a stoplight when Liza suddenly shouted, "SHIT!" And turned toward the back. "I just thought of something," Liza said. "What if we didn't win?" She looked kind of horrified. "We're acting like we won, we're just assuming Gil was first. She was fast. Someone could have been faster."

"Don't be ridiculous." Gil's voice was hard. She sounded almost angry. "No one could have beaten me." But the look in her eyes said that this hadn't occurred to her either. And now she was worried.

"We'll find out when we get back," Olivia said. "Either the council will be there or they won't." But she turned down the volume on the radio, and she did not sing along with any songs after that.

Lucy leaned back against her seat and watched as the sky darkened. Fat raindrops began to fall onto her skin, into her hair. Olivia did not pull over to put the top up, and no one asked her to. They just kept going like that, the top down, the rain pounding down into the car, drenching all of them.

A shimmering gold balloon was hovering in front of the door when they got back to Olivia's. Olivia reached out to touch it and it popped, releasing the faintest wisp of silver smoke. In the smoke were the faces of Olivia's Heartbreaker friends from SoundWave, smiling and waving while giving the finger.

Olivia shook her head.

It was just after midnight when they walked into the house. Usually when they were all together, Lucy felt like they were a part of something—even if Liza was crazy sometimes, and Olivia could be hard to read, Lucy felt like they were a unit and she was part of that. But now, as they made their way into Olivia's living room that night, Lucy could feel the vast distance between them, as though each one was sealed inside her own bubble with her own thoughts, floating off into space, all on her own.

Olivia stood in the living room, staring at the photograph of her grandmother that hung over the fireplace. She turned to face them.

"I'm making hot chocolate," she said. "Does anyone want hot chocolate?"

Gil and Lucy exchanged a look, and then Gil nodded. "Yeah," she said. "Okay." And she forced her mouth into a smile.

Lucy said, "Me too."

Liza licked her lips with her pointy cat tongue. "Same," she said.

They followed Olivia into the kitchen and sat at the thick wooden farm table while Olivia got glass bottles of milk and cream from the huge brushed-steel fridge. She heated the milk and cream together, then melted in two bars of dark chocolate, the warm sweet scent filling the air. They were all silent as Olivia whisked the mixture until it was frothy and then poured it into four off-white mugs and topped each with a drop of bourbon, then whipped cream and chocolate shavings. Lucy looked around. How strange it seemed that Olivia had so much actual food in there—a fully stocked pantry, breads in bags dusted with flour, a refrigerator filled with cheeses and piles of fruit, like a still-life painting come to life.

Olivia set the four mugs down on the table, one in front of each of them. Lucy reached for hers, too tired even to drink it. She just sat and let the sweet steam rise up toward her face.

For a while it felt like the four of them were together again—for a while it felt certain that everything would be okay. But time kept passing, and the Heartbreaker Council didn't appear. And with each hour that went by it seemed less and less likely that they were going to.

Twenty

Lucy and Gil lay back on the green velvet couches. It was four a.m. They were the only ones left awake.

"Are you sure you don't want to just head up to bed?" Gil asked for the third time in the last hour. "I'll wake you up when they get here, I promise." Gil's phone buzzed with a text. She looked down. "Beacon again," she said.

Lucy shook her head. "I'm not sleeping until they either come or . . ." She stopped. She could not allow herself to entertain any "or"s. Of course they were coming. They had to.

"I'm staying up with you." Lucy tried to smile. But for some reason Lucy's own friendliness felt forced now. They were supposed to be in this together, the two of them more than anyone. So why didn't it feel like that?

Lucy wasn't sure how much time had passed when she woke up on the couch, but there was Gil silhouetted in front of the window, typing furiously into her phone. She stopped. It vibrated. Gil read whatever was on the screen, let out a sigh, and then tiptoed out of the room. A minute later, Lucy heard the front door opening and then being slowly shut.

Lucy crept out of the living room into the hallway.

"No, absolutely not," Lucy heard Gil's voice say.

The heavy front door was opened just a crack. Lucy peeked through.

Gil was standing on the front steps with a girl. She was a Heartbreaker—Lucy could tell that right away, from her golden glow, from the tattoo on her chest. Was this girl part of the council? She had streaky blonde hair, tan skin, a wild look in her eyes. She looked familiar, and it only took a second for Lucy to realize why. Lucy had seen the girl in Alex's photographs from over the summer. *This was the Heartbreaker who'd broken his heart.*

Lucy leaned toward the door.

". . . that's not what we agreed on," Gil said. She sounded upset.

"But that was before things changed," the girl said.

"What do you want, Shay?"

This was Shay?

"I did you a favor, and now I want you to do me one. . . ."

"You didn't do me a favor, I paid you. The deal is done."

"The deal *was* done. And then I heard a rumor that you broke one of the HHB's hearts, and now I just can't help but feel you may be in a better position to do favors than you were before. . . ."

"Go home," said Gil. "We don't know if we won or not. And even if we did, you're not getting anything else."

"Are you sure?" Shay raised her eyebrows. "How do you think your sweet little sister Lucy would feel if she found out what you did? We all know you can't get into the prizes without all four of you."

"I didn't do anything," said Gil.

"Really? So it's just a coincidence that the guy whose heart you hired me to break just so happens to be the guy who broke the heart of your brand-new sister?"

Lucy's heart was pounding so hard she could barely breathe.

"Go ahead and tell Lucy whatever you want." Gil's voice wavered. "She already knows."

Shay laughed. "Really? And that's why you've been hiding from me for days?"

"I haven't been . . . ," Gil started. "I've been busy."

"*Ssh.*" Shay raised her finger to her lips. Behind it she smiled a sly-looking little smile. She just looked so pleased with herself, this girl who had stolen Alex away. Lucy thought she didn't care anymore. She *didn't* care anymore, not about the Alex part, at least. And yet . . .

Lucy felt her hand reaching for the knob, twisting it, pushing the door open. She stepped outside into the cool blue light of morning.

"Oh, hey girls," Lucy said easily, as though they were expecting her. Lucy slung one arm around Gil's shoulders. "You're Shay, right? Thanks, by the way, for what you did. To Alex, I mean." Lucy stuck out her hand.

Shay stared at her, her expression completely unreadable. She reached out. They shook—how weird it was to touch this girl who had touched Alex in ways Lucy never had.

Lucy took her hand away and wiped it on her pants as if she'd just touched something disgusting. "Nice try, by the way. But what Gilly says is completely true. I do know everything. I doubt the council will be very happy to hear about your attempts at blackmail. And they'll be here any minute, so . . ." Lucy steeled her jaw and stared at Shay. "You probably shouldn't be."

Shay tipped her head to the side, bit her lip coyly, then shrugged and sighed. "Well, damn." She grinned at both of them. "It never hurts to try, right?" Shay slowly looked Lucy up and down. "I don't know how you put up with him as long as you did, really. He was so needy. And awful in bed too. Just"—she held up her pinky—"awful."

Shay made her way down the steps, walked to the driveway,

got in a little yellow car, and drove away.

Gil turned toward Lucy. "I don't even know what to say." Her lip was trembling, her mouth curled into a grateful smile.

Lucy shook her head. "Just explain." Her voice was an ice-cold whisper. "What the hell was she talking about?" Lucy felt the tears begin to form behind her eyelids, but they didn't fall. She was too angry.

"I just . . ." Gil looked panicked, like she was trying very hard to come up with a suitable answer.

"Tell me the truth," Lucy said.

"The truth is . . ." Gil turned away. "The truth is, I bribed her to take Alex from you." Her voice was so quiet, Lucy could barely hear her.

"I don't understand."

"Last year, remember how you and me and Alex were all in that same American History class? It was already obvious that you were in love with him—anyone could have seen that. But I was using the Love Lines potion one day, and I saw that he didn't love you back. And he was never going to." Gil cleared her throat. "He was so cocky and really kind of a jerk, but you just couldn't see it. And then we did that thing in class where everyone talked about our summer plans, and Alex kept bragging about going to Colorado and I knew Shay lived there, so I asked her to . . . to take care of it."

Lucy pressed her fist to her chest. "So in a way, you could say that *you* broke my heart."

Gil reached out for Lucy's hand. But Lucy pulled away. "But you don't understand," Gil said. "It would have happened anyway, don't you see? The stuff with Shay just made it happen sooner."

Lucy took a breath. "Does Olivia know? And Liza? Were they in on it too?"

Gil shook her head. "It was just me."

Lucy felt like she was sinking into something thick and dark. "Is this why you 'helped' me when I was trying to get Alex back? Because you knew it wouldn't work and I'd be even more heartbroken, and you'd be there to pick up the pieces?"

Gil looked down and didn't answer.

"How much of this did you plan? *Did you know I was going to break Tristan's heart?*" Lucy was almost shouting now. She felt hot and sick inside. She could barely breathe.

Gil looked small and scared. She said nothing.

Lucy pushed past her, felt her legs walking her down the front steps, out onto the driveway, trying to take her away from all of this.

"Lucy, wait, WAIT!" She could hear Gil's footsteps behind her. "I couldn't have known you were going to break Tristan's heart. I don't know the future. No one does. Yes, I saw that he was in love with you. But I wasn't sure *what* would happen. We didn't force you to become one of us, Lucy, and we never could have. *You* chose to do that."

Lucy pressed her lips together and felt her heart thunk. She had thought no one could ever hurt her more than Alex had when he broke up with her, and no one could betray her worse than he did when he let her pine away for him all summer long without ever telling her the truth. But as it turned out, she'd been wrong. Gil wasn't just some idiot guy who'd made a cowardly mistake. Gil was supposed to be someone she could trust, someone she could count on. Gil was supposed to be her sister.

"What was real, then?" said Lucy. "Was any of this? *Sister?*" She sneered when she said the word.

"My friendship, Lucy, that's real. And I really do consider you my sister. I did right from the very beginning."

"Well, it makes sense that you only have brothers, then."

"You don't understand," Gil said. "I had to do it."

Lucy felt empty. And so entirely alone. "No one has to do anything," she said. She turned to go.

"Please, Lucy," Gil said. "Wait!"

"Why? You're worried if I leave and we win, you won't be able to get into your precious prizes?"

"No, that's not it," said Gil. And then she paused. She looked down at the ground. And when she spoke again, she sounded desperate. "If you leave, if we don't get the Diamonding Powder, *Liza's mother will probably die.*"

Lucy stopped. She felt a chill run through her. "What are you talking about?"

"Liza's mom is more messed up than I've told you," Gil said. "More messed up than Liza will admit. Liza's mom tried to kill herself a couple months ago." Gil's voice wavered. "And it wasn't the first time either. She tries all the time. But it's like I told you, she's a Glass Heart. Of course, *Glass Heart* isn't something any doctor is ever going to understand. No matter how many therapists she sees or pills she takes, it won't help. The Diamonding Powder is the only thing I've ever heard of that could help her. It's pretty much her only chance."

Lucy's head was spinning. She had no idea what to think, what to believe. "Why didn't you tell me this before?"

"Because you already feel responsible for Tristan. That's enough."

"But why are you the one doing this? Why isn't Liza? Why isn't Olivia helping?"

"Olivia's parents are already dead. I can't even talk to her about this. And Liza?" Gil shook her head. "She's in complete denial about it. You've seen how she gets. But I can't just sit by and watch my friend's mother die. Could you? What if it was Tristan's mom? If she was still alive and he couldn't face the truth. Wouldn't you do anything at all to spare him the pain of losing her?" She paused. "We are so, so lucky to get to be who we are. But that doesn't mean we can just sit by and watch other people suffer. . . ." Gil stopped then. She took a breath. "But that's only part of why I did what I did."

"Go on." Lucy held her breath.

"Lucy, you weren't the only girl we could have chosen to become one of us. It would have been easy to find someone else. I picked you because I knew you were special from the moment I met you, even before we ever spoke. I picked you because you seemed so kind and sweet, and I hated to imagine you having to suffer heartbreak at all, let alone more than once. I saw you with Alex, the way you looked at him with your soft breakable heart, and I thought, I have to help this girl. She deserves the freedom that I have. She deserves to believe in magic and have that belief proved true." Gil stopped then and looked Lucy straight in the eye. "And I am so sorry for what I did. But only for the lying part. Not for the rest of it. And if you can forgive me, I swear I will never, ever lie to you again."

Gil still held Lucy's gaze. And Lucy felt her insides softening, the anger draining out of her. Everything Gil said made sense. She couldn't quite feel it in her heart, but in her ears and in her mind, the truth of it was clear.

"Please, Lucy," Gil said. She held out her hand.

This was Gil, her friend. Her sister. She'd done a good

thing in a less-than-honest way. But in the end, Gil had given Lucy an amazing gift. And she wanted to give an amazing gift to others.

"Okay," Lucy said quietly. "Okay." She reached out and took it.

Back inside, the hallway smelled different—like forest and rushing water. And the air felt strange and heavy like it does right before a storm. Before Lucy could process what was going on, Gil was running toward the stairs, cupping her hands around her mouth. "OLIVIA! LIZA! COME DOWN! WE WON!!" she shouted.

And then Lucy saw it—in the center of the room was a trunk made of blue stained glass in every shade from sky to midnight. On the side of the chest was a broken heart in deep bloodred.

Her breath caught in her throat. They'd actually done it. They'd won. And because of that, Tristan had won too. And his prize would be a brand-new heart. The suffering she'd caused him would be over so soon now. Lucy felt a prickling behind her eyelids and pressed her hand to her chest.

"Wait!" Olivia came racing down the stairs, eyes wild, hair streaming. She ran to the front door. The rest of them followed.

"Wait!!" she shouted again. She flung the door open and stared out into the night. But all that was there was the moon glowing dully behind clouds, the trees, and the road, which was empty. Olivia stood there, breathing heavily. Then she walked back inside.

"They were here," Olivia said, her voice quiet. "But they're gone now."

Liza was standing in the living room, staring down at the box. "So *what*?" she said. "They left the prizes." Her lips spread into a satisfied smile, as though somehow she alone was responsible for all of this.

"No, you're right." Olivia turned away, then said so quietly Lucy could barely hear her, "I just wanted to ask them something, I guess." Olivia bent down and ran her hand along the top of the glass chest. There was a gold heart inlaid into each corner.

"Well," Olivia said. "Let's open it up, then, shall we?"

She placed one palm over one of the hearts, and the other over her tattoo. Liza followed, and so did Gil.

"Lucy?" Gil said. "We need you for this. . . ." There was a hint of nervousness in her voice, like she wasn't quite sure what Lucy would do.

Lucy knelt down, then put one hand on the box and the other over her heart. She waited; she breathed in. For a moment she was paralyzed. She felt a jolt of electricity go through her. And then the lock on the box popped open.

A curl of smoke escaped and twisted itself into words: *Careful, now. . . .*

Olivia lifted the lid. There in the center of the chest was a book bound in cracked brown leather, the cover embossed with intricate gold swirls.

"*The Book of Love*," Olivia whispered.

Olivia lifted it out of the box. It was enormous, a foot wide and a foot and a half long and eight or nine inches thick. Her arms shook from the sheer weight of it. She placed it on the table in front of them.

Liza reached out and ran her hand over the cover. "That is so beautiful," she said.

But while Olivia and Liza were staring at the book, Gil was staring at something else. Right there in a pocket at the side of the box was a small gold vial, shaped like the head of an Egyptian goddess. In place of one eye was a tiny glittering diamond.

"Wow," Gil said. "That's just incredible. . . ." She leaned over the book, and all the while she was sliding her hand into the box and curling her fingers around the goddess. She slipped it into her palm, and no one saw but Lucy. Lucy's heart let out a thud.

Gil looked up and locked eyes with Lucy. She let the side of her mouth curve into a smirk, and then she held one finger up to her lips. *Ssh.*

"I wonder what else is in here," Gil said. She gazed down into the chest as though for the very first time and started pulling out the potions one by one.

There was a small crystal jar filled with brightly colored petals marked *Forget-Me Flowers*; black powder inside a glittery stone box labeled *Destiny Dust*; a little perfume atomizer with a ruby stopper and a tag reading *Déjà View*. And that was just the beginning. By the time the chest was empty, there were dozens of powders, potions, and elixirs laid out on the floor.

But Olivia was still staring at the book. "Okay," she whispered. "Here we go." She lifted the cover and turned to the first page. The paper was thick and rough and slightly yellowed around the edges. *The Book of Love* was written in gold ink. She flipped to the next page, where there was a short paragraph written in black:

> *We the elite Heartbreakers who have been granted access to this book, the pages of which have been sprinkled with tears and drenched in wisdom, vow to keep what we read here locked within the fortresses of our locked-up hearts.*

And below that were dozens of names arranged into columns.

"Hey," Gil said. "Your granny is on here." She pointed to *Eleanor de Lune* written out in beautiful swooping script.

Olivia pressed her lips together, then shrugged. She flipped to a page in the middle of the book, and they all leaned over her shoulder and read.

On Breaking the Heart of a Prince
Jane Caldwell, 1882

As Prince Philippe made his way into the ballroom, all the ladies of the court turned to stare, and a dozen cheeks burned with the first blooms of sudden fierce desire. His height, his broad chest, that lavish silver brocade waistcoat, his jet-black hair swept back from his high forehead, he was a rare sight to behold and he knew it. He smiled that day, courteously, modestly even. But I knew his modesty was as much a lie as any of the thousands of others that would soon spill from his marble-carved lips. When our eyes met, his revealed him to be the owner of a cruel and callous heart, a heart that had never been humbled. Well, I thought to myself, we'll soon fix that. . . .

The entry went on for four more pages, chronicling the Heartbreaker's courtship with the prince, the tactics she used to woo him and break him, and what she did with his tears when she was done.

Olivia flipped to the next entry—a courtesan's account of breaking the heart of a wealthy merchant. And then the next—a muse's account of breaking the famous artist who sculpted her. And so on and so on. The pages were packed with wisdom, spelled out in curling script or scratchy print, in black, gray, and shimmering gold ink. There were scented pages, and pages containing tiny drawings the Heartbreakers had done of their conquests; there were entries that explained the truth behind historical fictions accepted as facts, and the truth behind facts believed to be fiction, as well as recipes for hundreds of potions, powders, elixirs, and charms.

Gil was holding the book now, flipping from page to page, reading the names of some of the entries out loud. " 'Getting Straight to the Heart of Archduke Ferdinand. I Was the One Who Left Charlie Chaplin Speechless. On Bringing an Astronaut Back Down to Earth. Charm for Erasing Yourself from a Memory. Charm for Inserting Yourself into a Memory. How to Cheat a Cheater. On the Eve of . . .' " Gil looked up. "Hey, wait a second. Olivia. This one is by your grandmother. . . ."

"And what did Eleanor have to say for herself?" Olivia said quietly. Her eyelid twitched. The rest of her face remained expressionless.

Gil began to read. " 'I have never regretted my choice, and today of all days, I am especially grateful for my solid unbreakable heart. Earlier this evening I got a call from the hospital telling me that . . .' " Gil stopped and looked up. "Oh," she said. She pressed her lips together.

"Go on," said Olivia.

Gil took a breath. " 'I got a call from the hospital telling me that my daughter and son-in-law were killed in an accident. They were driving home from a party, and their car was hit head-on. They died painlessly, instantly, or so I've been told.

I was never able to protect my daughter—she never wanted me to, even in the ways that I could have. But today our magic protects my heart, now when I need it more than ever. Tomorrow their daughter, Olivia, who will soon be thirteen . . ."

"Okay," Olivia said. She cleared her throat. "Enough." She reached out and took the book from Gil's lap. Then she closed it up, sealing the past inside. "We're tired and it's late," she said. "No more of this now."

Olivia picked up the book and carried it to the stairs. But before Olivia started to climb, Lucy caught a glimpse of her face twisted into an expression that Lucy had never seen her make before, and could not even begin to understand.

Twenty-One

♥

Lucy woke up alone. It felt like the middle of the night, but the sun streaming through the sheer curtains told her it was morning, and the clock by the bed read 9:15. She stared across the room at a queen bed, identical to the one she was in. It was empty, perfectly made, as though Gil had never been there at all.

Just a few hours before, they'd finally made their way up to the guest room they usually shared when they both stayed over Olivia's house. Lucy had assumed she and Gil would have a final chat about everything that had happened, about Shay and the amazing book, and about the Diamonding

Powder and their plans for it. Lucy herself was so confused and so tired she didn't even know where to begin. But when she got back from brushing her teeth, Gil was already asleep with a tiny diamond peeking out from her clenched fist.

Now Lucy lay in bed going over the events of the past couple of days on her own—the makeover, the trip to SoundWave, seeing Tristan with Phee, meeting Beacon, performing at the festival, finding out Gil had lied and then finding out why. She couldn't begin to wrap her head around any of it.

Least of all, this: Today was the day she was going to fix Tristan's heart. She finally could. And she could fix it forever. All the longing and pain and need he'd ever felt would be just a memory. He would be like her, free and unbreakable for the rest of his life.

Lucy sat up, pulled back the curtains, and looked out onto a beautiful fall day. Tristan probably wouldn't be back from the festival until sometime in the afternoon, and Olivia and Liza wouldn't be up for hours. And who even knew where Gil was. That was okay. There was no rush now.

Lucy yawned and stretched and padded down the hallway into the grand marble bathroom. She turned the gold faucets and stepped into the marble shower. She heard the door open and through the fogged-up glass saw a figure walk into the bathroom. It was around the size and shape of Gil.

"Gil? Hello?" Lucy called out into the steamy air. But no one answered. And by the time she got out of the shower, the room was empty. In the center of the marble counter was that tiny gold goddess head and a little slip of a note.

Took what I needed. The rest is for you. Don't open the bottle until you're ready to use it. Magic this strong tends to have a way of escaping. xx G

Lucy squeezed the tiny bottle in her fist.

She took it back to the room and set it on the dresser. She stared at it as she dried herself off and changed into a pair of dark jeans and a soft tangerine sweater that she found in her SoundWave bag. It was just after ten. Now what?

Well, one thing was for certain—she couldn't stay here, not with this incredibly powerful magic that, if they found out about, Olivia and Liza would most certainly want back.

And with that realization, Lucy felt a rush of anxious energy shoot up her spine. She tucked the bottle into her pocket and went down to Olivia's kitchen and packed up some food—sharp cheddar and tomatoes on toasted sourdough bread, a perfectly ripe pear, a bottle of water, and a handful of chocolate-covered almonds. And then she walked outside. She had an amazing day ahead of her.

She'd never pedaled harder when she hit the road.

Twenty-Two

♥

S o, you may want to consider adding psychic to your list of skills, bud," Tristan said, by way of greeting. It was hours later, and Tristan was standing in his doorway, barefoot in jeans and a gray T-shirt, face scrubbed and hair damp like he'd just gotten out of the shower. "Because I literally just got home a few minutes ago and was literally just about to call you. Literally." He grinned.

"Really? Literally?" said Lucy.

"Also figuratively," he said.

And Lucy laughed. The truth was, she'd been riding around his neighborhood for the past hour. She'd finally seen his truck in the driveway and had forced herself to ride for ten more minutes before she rang his bell, to steady her nerves.

"Well, come in, then." Tristan led her into his house and up to his room. "Stay here," he said. "I'll be back in a sec."

Lucy sat at Tristan's desk and looked around. She'd always liked his bedroom. Tristan's truck was a crazy chaotic jumble of stuff: lollipop sticks, empty coffee cups, harmonicas, a box of old glass seltzer bottles rescued from the side of the road, a big inflatable deer head, which sometimes rode shotgun, and for a while he'd even had a popcorn popper that he plugged into the cigarette lighter. His truck was fun, but it wasn't exactly soothing.

His room, however, was a whole different thing.

It was clean, calm, and uncluttered with a light wood floor, mint green walls, and an olive striped comforter. But there were still charming bits of Tristanliness: an old map was hung up on the wall decorated in hand-drawn sea monsters (which Tristan had obviously added himself), a vintage harmonica collection sat on his desk, and at one end of the bookshelf there was a glass apothecary jar containing nothing but a tiny plastic cow. She'd once asked him what it was. "Oh that," he'd said, completely deadpan. "That's my experiment."

It had been months since Lucy had been in here, but the room smelled exactly the way it always had—like pine trees, apples, and earth.

"Okay! Get ready for ultimate refreshment," Tristan shouted

from the hall. He walked in carrying two frosty glasses and handed one to Lucy. "Homemade limeade. Squozen with my very own hands."

Lucy sipped her limeade. It was tart and cool, and in theory she knew it was delicious, but somehow it felt as though someone else's mouth was drinking it.

"It's my new favorite thing," Tristan said. "Making it is like working out with one of those hand-exercise ball thingies, but then your prize at the end is a delicious drink." He took another gulp. "So," he said. "Did you have fun at the show? You left the concert so fast we didn't really get to say good-bye."

"Sorry about that. My friends wanted to leave . . . ," Lucy said. "Phee seems nice. . . ." She smiled, then squeezed the tiny vial in her pocket. Her heart was hammering. "Did you guys have a good time?"

Tristan nodded. "Yeah, an excellent time. Phee actually ended up hooking up with one of the guys from that band Offshore, so she was pretty excited."

Lucy ran her thumbnail over the tiny diamond.

"Oh," said Lucy. "I thought maybe you two were . . ." Lucy stopped herself. It wasn't her business. And it shouldn't matter now anyway.

"Together? Nah, we're just buds."

And Lucy felt a rush of something along her spine. What was it exactly? Relief is what it felt like, probably because if he were dating Phee and Lucy fixed his heart, it would just mean another person would get hurt. It was easier this way. Simpler.

"Okay," Lucy said. "It just kind of seemed like she liked you."

"Well, I guess she did at first." Tristan coughed. "But I'm not up for anything right now, so I told her that. And then actually stuck to it." Tristan gave Lucy a wry smile. "I used to think that when I told a girl I wasn't looking for a relationship, it meant I was freed from all responsibility. So then if we hooked up and she wanted me to be her boyfriend and her feelings got hurt, I'd think, 'Well, yeah, but I warned her,' as though somehow saying that made it fair. Which is completely wrong, obviously." Tristan shook his head. "It's just easy to believe your own lies. But I'm not doing that anymore." Tristan smiled. "And there ends Tristan's self-discovery hour." He laughed. "Sorry for being all weird lately." He drained his glass and put it down on the nightstand. "I've just been . . . thinking about a lot of stuff these past few weeks." And he looked at her. He pushed his damp hair back from his forehead.

Was it time yet? Should she do it now? "That's not a bad thing," said Lucy.

"No," said Tristan. "I don't guess it is." Then Tristan took a breath. He leaned forward, put his elbows on his knees. "Luce," Tristan said. "The reason I was going to call you is because I actually need to talk to you about something and it's a little bit serious." He pushed his hair away from his forehead. "I know things have been kind of funny between us lately, and we haven't really talked about why. But I guess what I wanted to say is that it is completely my fault."

"No, it's not," Lucy said quickly. "I've been—"

"Just let me explain, please, okay? I tried to tell you something a couple of months ago, right after you broke up with Alex. But I had really terrible selfish timing, so it didn't happen then. And I've tried to tell you other times too, the other night in my truck when you called me, and a dozen times before that." He paused and smiled. "I'm sorry, I don't mean to be so cryptic. You probably have no idea what I'm talking about. . . ."

Lucy looked down. Of course, she did have an idea—in fact she knew exactly what he was about to say. But he didn't need to make any painful embarrassing confessions, because in a minute, the thing he was about to confess wouldn't even be true anymore. Once she fixed his heart, he'd be free of all of this. Should she stop him? She held the magic in her hand.

"I know that once these words are out, I can't take them back," Tristan said. "And I know it will change things. But I guess even unsaid, it already has, so . . ."

"Wait!"

But he didn't. He took a breath. He looked brave. He lifted his head up and looked her right in the eye. "Lucy, I love you."

Lucy raised her hand to her lips. And even though none of this was news, she still felt surprised, surprised that they were having this conversation at all.

"Wait, before you try and say anything, I guess I might as well tell you I have kind of felt this since we first started being friends. I mean, I wasn't aware of it the entire time, but it was always there. And it was only when you started dating Alex that I really admitted it to myself, and I thought I'd just forget about it, let it go, ignore it 'til it faded, only then your friend Gil said something once, just this offhand thing that made me think that maybe . . ." He paused and stared down at his glass.

"Maybe what?" Lucy's heart was hammering.

"Never mind."

"Please," said Lucy. *What had Gil said?*

Tristan shook his head. "It's not important anymore because she was wrong." He looked back up and their eyes met again. "What's important is I guess just that I'm telling you. Because . . . I just needed you to know."

Lucy nodded. She lowered her hand to her chest.

"Well, thank you for telling me," Lucy said. "But you don't have to worry, I can fix your heart." The words popped out, and she heard them as she said them. She hadn't meant to tell him. She was just supposed to do it. "I . . ." She stopped. He was shaking his head.

Tristan laughed softly. "I'm pretty sure time will be the

one in charge of that," he said. "That's how it's supposed to work. And that's okay. It's . . . maybe it's not even such a bad thing, right? I'll have inspiration for a million terrible poems after this. It's just too bad more things don't rhyme with your name." He grinned sweetly. "But Lucy," he said. He sounded, just then, so very sorry. "Here's the thing. You're really lovely to want to help, I mean, it's part of why I feel the way I do, I suppose. But I think, this is really hard to say, maybe even harder than what I just said, but I think I probably need to stop pretending that I can be friends with you. At least for right now." There was no bitterness in his voice. He wasn't trying to hurt her or punish her. All he was doing was telling the truth.

And then Tristan stood. Lucy stood too. Her entire body was tingling. She pulled the vial from her pocket and held it at her hip. She stared down at the tiny winking diamond eye. It was now or never. It was time. She started to uncap the vial, but before she could, she felt arms around her, felt Tristan leaning in for a hug.

"I'm really sorry," he said. "I hope you can understand."

She could feel the warmth of his skin through his thin shirt. And without thinking, she let her body melt into it. They had hugged before, of course, they had hugged a million times, but it had never been like this, their entire bodies lining up from head to toe. She could feel his belly against her belly and his hands on her back. She could hear his breath in her ear, feel his heart against her cheek.

"Tris . . . ," Lucy started to say. There was heat passing between them. She could feel him warming up her insides, her cold heart. She tipped her head back and looked up at him, his face lit by the afternoon sun.

And then, before Lucy knew what was happening, he was inching toward her, closer and closer until finally their lips were touching.

His mouth was soft. He tasted like sugar and limes.

She could feel his hands on her back, resting so lightly as though at any moment she might try to run away, and he would not try to stop her.

But she was not running. She was kissing him back. It was gentle at first, chaste and sweet. Then she felt his tongue in her mouth, and she reached her hand up and held the back of his neck. And for a split second all there was were her lips and his lips and their hands and tongues. And she was just *there*, wholly and completely in that perfect luminous moment with no future and no past, only here, now, this.

But then the thoughts started rolling in.

This was Tristan, her best friend whose heart she had broken, her best friend who *loved* her. She could not keep kissing him if she could not promise him her heart. But her heart wasn't hers to give anymore. And wasn't she supposed to be fixing his?

What was she doing?

Lucy stepped back. She stared at him, blinking.

But Tristan didn't look upset. He just nodded and put his hands in his pockets. He seemed, if not happy exactly, at least somehow free. And Lucy realized then what he'd been doing when he kissed her—he hadn't been making one final attempt, hoping that somehow things could be different between them. No. What he'd been doing was kissing her good-bye.

Lucy stared at him. She squeezed the little gold vial in her fist. But she knew she wasn't going to use the Diamonding Powder that day, not then, not on him. It wouldn't be fair. It wasn't what he wanted.

"I should go now," Lucy said.

Tristan nodded. He walked her downstairs, and then he stood there waving in the doorway while she pedaled away, waving like she was already gone.

Twenty-Three

♥

What the hell had just happened?

Lucy's head was spinning. Her legs were exhausted, but she forced them to go.

Lucy had never liked Tristan as anything more than a friend. In all the years of knowing him, it had never even occurred to her that he would ever be anything but one. When he'd first tried to confess his love for her almost two months ago, she had been scared—scared that, if he did, nothing would ever be the same between them. And so she'd stopped him from telling her. But what if instead . . . she'd let him?

No! Lucy tried to shake her head, to shake the thoughts out. Why was she thinking about all of this now? When it was far too late for anything to ever happen?

And *why couldn't she stop feeling his lips on hers?*

Lucy lifted herself off the seat so she was standing, still pedaling. She felt the small gold vial pressing against her leg inside her pocket. The Diamonding Powder. The magic she so badly wanted but now couldn't even use. She should go to Gil and she should give it back.

And then a thought popped into Lucy's head. What Tristan had said, about Gil. He confessed his love to Lucy because of something Gil said.

Gil said something. . . .

But what?

Lucy's heart pounded along with her fist as she rapped on Gil's front door. She could hear sounds coming from inside— music, a TV sitcom with a heavy laugh track. She felt strange and fuzzy, like she was trapped behind glass, like the fear she was feeling was not even her own.

Lucy knocked again, harder this time.

The door swung open, and a girl popped her head out. She looked vaguely familiar, but Lucy was pretty sure she'd never actually met her before. It would be impossible to forget someone this stunning. The girl's skin was flawless, her eyes were fringed in thick lashes, her hair was lush, and her lips were pursed into a Cupid's bow, both sexy and sweet. Everything about this girl was perfect except better, because perfection gets boring, and this girl had the sort of face you could stare at forever. Lucy blinked. She forced herself to look away.

"Hi," Lucy said. "Is Gil here?"

The girl's mouth spread into a luminous smile and she laughed. Lucy knew that laugh.

"Luce, it's *me*!" The girl threw her arms up in the air and did a twirl. "Gilly-bean!"

Lucy stared at the girl. "I don't understand," said Lucy. "What happened?"

"Magic!" Gil said. She stuck out her hip, waiting for Lucy to react. But Lucy didn't say anything—she didn't know what to say. Gil pushed her lips into a pout. "Okay, fine. I'm sorry."

"For what?"

"For what you're here about."

"I don't understand."

Gil narrowed her eyes. "You mean you don't know?"

"Don't know what?"

"Have you been to see Tristan yet?"

"That's why I'm here."

"So then you know what I did."

"You mean what you said?"

"What I said when?"

"Wait, what are we talking about?"

Gil laughed again. "I don't know, Luce, why don't you tell me."

"I went to see Tristan," Lucy said. "I was planning to use the powder on him. But I ended up not doing it. It didn't seem right."

"Okay, fine," she said. She looked, Lucy thought, the tiniest bit relieved. "But then what's the problem?"

Lucy closed her eyes. She could feel Tristan's arms around her. She opened her eyes and looked at Gil. "Tristan told me that he'd been planning to let his feelings for me fade, that he was just going to ignore them until they went away, but then something *you* said made him change his mind. So what I want to know is, what was it? What did you tell him?"

Gil shrugged. "I just told him the truth."

"The truth about what?"

"The truth about you and him," Gil said slowly. "That you could fall in love with him." Gil smirked. "Well, not anymore, of course, but, you know, back then."

Lucy's heart lurched and she felt the ground shift beneath her feet. "That doesn't even make any sense," she said. Lucy had a sudden urge to reach out and grab Gil. To shake her and shake her until that pleased little smile shook loose from her face. "You're lying."

Gil shook her head. "People lie. But magic never does. You remember how I said I was using the Love Lines potion, and that's how I found out that Alex would never love you back? Tristan came to meet you after class that day, and I saw everything. It was just lucky, I guess."

"Lucky?"

"For you, because you got to be a Heartbreaker. And then, of course, lucky for me because . . ." Gil gestured toward her face.

"And how exactly did that happen?" Lucy asked.

Gil pursed her lips, opened her eyes wide, and looked up to the side in mock innocence. "I don't know, Lucy. You tell me."

"How can I tell you?" Lucy said. "I don't even know what's going on." Only then, all at once, she did. "Olivia said Diamonding Powder was supposed to be as versatile as a diamond. It could be used to give someone a diamond-strong heart . . ."

"Or," Gil finished, "a diamond's beauty."

Hands shaking, Lucy pulled the goddess head out of her pocket, the vial she'd been so carefully guarding. She pulled the stopper out and stared down into the little golden space.

There was nothing there.

"Oh my god," Lucy whispered. She looked up.

"I'm sorry, Lu," Gil said. But she didn't even bother trying to sound it.

"I broke Colin's heart for *this*? So you could become really *pretty*?" Lucy leaned against the door frame. Her body did not want to hold her up anymore. "When you left the vial while I was in the shower, had you . . ."

"It was already starting to do its thing," Gil said, nodding. "But I needed to make sure no one saw me because it hadn't finished taking effect. And at that point someone still could have stopped me."

Lucy could barely breathe. "Did you ever actually plan on helping anyone?"

Gil rolled her eyes. "Does it matter?"

Lucy blinked. "You're like an entirely different person," she said. "It's not just the looks. You don't even seem like you anymore."

"I guess all that stuff they say about it being dangerous to leave one person alone with too much power is kinda true." She let out a laugh. "I really did want to help Liza's sad mommy, at first. Okay? But then I spent all that time with Beacon. And I just started thinking, well, *why*? *She is* sad, sure, but whose fault was that really?"

"You said it was no one's fault," Lucy said.

"Well, what do I know? I worked *hard* for this. I earned it!" Gil paused. "Look, I know that you probably feel a little annoyed right now, but I'll make it up to you, okay? I realize I wouldn't have been able to do any of this without you, and I haven't forgotten that. Next time you want a couple of extra tear vials, you just let me know. I'll tell you how to break into the safe." Gil smiled at Lucy. It was not a cruel smile or a spiteful smile. It was just a smile that said, *I've gotten what I wanted. And nothing else matters.* "Besides, you didn't even want to use the powder on Tristan anyway. So it's really no biggie, right?"

Gil stood staring at her, waiting for an answer. But Lucy just shook her head, picked up her bike, and climbed on.

Lucy knew what she should be feeling at that moment—what the old Lucy would have felt: anger, sadness, fear, regret, worry—but instead, she felt nothing but the wind on her cheeks and deep in her gut the slightest tickle of understanding that maybe somewhere along the way she had made a giant unfixable mistake.

Twenty-Four

♥

Lucy was home.

The lights were on inside. Lucy opened the door. The house was completely silent.

Lucy walked up the stairs, numb. She thought about how it had once seemed so wonderful that there was magic in the world, but she could not at that moment feel even a tiny shred of that delight.

At the top of the stairs Lucy realized her parents' door was open. They were inside, speaking quietly to each other. Lucy stood there for a minute, just staring. They were taking items out of her dad's dresser and putting them in suitcases.

"Maybe these should go in the bigger one," her mom said. She was holding up a pair of Lucy's father's khakis. "That way they won't get as wrinkled."

Her father nodded. "Thank you," he said. "That's a good idea." His voice sounded different than she had ever heard it. It was like she was watching strangers, strangers to herself and to each other.

Lucy knocked on the open door. Her parents turned in unison. Their eyes looked sad, and they both smiled these complicated smiles that Lucy did not understand.

"Hey, honey," said her mom.

Her dad said, "Come in for a minute." He pushed the door open wider. Lucy had a sudden crazy overwhelming urge to run, far away from them, from everyone and everything. She did not know where she would go, though, because, she realized as she stared at her parents, there *was* nowhere to go. There never was. Putting more space between her and this and whatever they were going to say next wouldn't make it less real—it wouldn't even make it further away. She'd bring all of it right along with her.

Lucy stepped inside. Her mom motioned, and Lucy sat in the chair by the window.

"We know we've said a number of times in the past . . . ," her dad started.

Her mom continued, ". . . so if you don't believe us at first, we understand."

"But we want you to know that we've had a long talk, and this time we're quite serious." Her dad was looking at her mom now.

And then they both nodded, looked straight at Lucy, and said, "We're getting divorced," her mother first and her father right after, their words overlapping.

Lucy felt nothing.

"Oh," Lucy said. "Wow."

What was she supposed to be feeling? Sadness? Anger? Relief? She tried to form her face to match the appropriate emotion. But inside, she was completely blank. She knew there was such a thing as shock, that sometimes when something really bad happened it took a while to sink in. When she was eight, she saw her neighbor's dog get hit by a car and die right in front of her house. She still remembered the yelp of pain, the helpless look in the dog's eyes, the feeling of floaty calm that overtook her as her mother rushed her inside, made her tea, wrapped her in a blanket as though she was the one who'd collided with that dark green station wagon. She had not felt anything, anything at all, until later that night in bed, when she started shaking and could not stop. She knew the detached self-protective calm that surrounds people after painful things happen. But this was not that—this was something else entirely.

"Are you okay?" Her mother came and put her arm around Lucy. Her father stood on the other side. "We know this must be a big surprise for you," her mother said. "I mean, the fact that we're actually doing this. But we got to talking the other night. We had an actual rational friendly discussion about this for the first time, well, maybe ever. And we realized it was just the best thing for everyone. . . ." She turned to Lucy's father, and he nodded.

"This was probably something we should have done a long time ago," her dad said. "We just couldn't quite figure out how. We hope you can understand." He smiled sadly.

"I can," Lucy said. "I mean, I agree with all of that." But her words sounded funny to her—like someone else was saying them.

Lucy's mom gave her a hug and then excused herself and went downstairs. Lucy sat there with her dad as he continued to pack. He was taking socks out of his drawer, balling them in pairs, and putting them in his suitcase. She watched as he paired up an unmatched set, one black, one navy. Lucy knew that this was the type of detail that would have wrecked her in the past, the idea of her dad, off on his own with his wrong socks, and no one to help him right them. But in that moment she felt only afraid. A brief flash of fear, and then nothing.

Twenty-Five

L ucy remembered the first time she'd stood outside these
enormous oak doors, when it had sounded as though
there was an entire ocean behind them and everything
that was about to happen hadn't happened yet. She remembered how scared she'd been then, how behind that fear there
was hope. But what about now? What did she feel? What was
left?

Lucy walked right in. Olivia was leaning back on a green
velvet couch, staring at an envelope.

Lucy didn't even wait for her to look up. "Did you know
Gil recruited me?"

Olivia smiled. "I'm sorry, what?"

"Gil. She hired a Heartbreaker to steal Alex."

"Well," she said. "No, I had not heard that before. I take it from your tone that this is a problem."

"Yes, it's a problem," Lucy said. And then Lucy told Olivia everything—about Shay, about Alex, about Tristan, about Gil and the Diamonding Powder and Liza's Glass Heart mother whom they'd been supposed to save.

Olivia swept her white blonde hair away from her face and turned toward the window. She looked, for a moment, almost upset. But then she simply said coolly, "There is no such thing as a Glass Heart."

Lucy blinked. "What do you mean?"

"Liza's mom is sick and her problems are complicated, but they're not *mystical*. She doesn't take the medication she should take and takes lots she shouldn't, and she drinks too much. But she has never tried to kill herself. You think if she had, Gil would be the only one doing anything about it?"

"Gil said . . ."

Olivia shook her head. "Gil can say whatever she wants. It doesn't change the truth."

"But Gil told me she was a Glass Heart before I was even a Heartbreaker."

"Well, I don't know," Olivia said. "Maybe she was planning something all along, or giving herself a good excuse in case you ever found out anything she didn't want you to know. . . ."

"Oh my god." Lucy stood there, arms frozen at her sides.

Olivia sighed. "So, it's not ideal. But what exactly do you expect me to do about it?"

"I don't know." Her voice was quiet. "But Gil has been keeping secrets this whole time, then!"

"Lucy," Olivia said. "Everyone has secrets."

"She tricked me to get me to join you."

"No, you *chose* to join us. If, at some point along the way, you misunderstood the reality of certain situations, that's no one's fault but your own." Olivia stopped then. Her jaw was set, and one of her eyelids twitched.

"But that's . . . ," Lucy started to say.

"Well, however you ended up joining, you're getting all the benefits from it anyway," Olivia said, more gently.

"What benefits?"

"When you're a Heartbreaker, life is just easier."

"I don't understand."

"Haven't you noticed how clean and simple things are starting to get? How with every day that passes, you become more untouchable?"

"Is that what this is? Why feelings aren't working right anymore?" Lucy's voice cracked.

"Working *right*?"

"Ever since I became a Heartbreaker, things have been . . .

they've just been wrong. I don't feel things the same way."

"Of course you don't." Olivia nodded. "There's a layer around your heart now. The more hearts you break, and the more magic you use, the thicker it gets."

"But that's awful." Lucy felt a tense buzzing in her chest.

"No, it's not." Olivia shook her head. "It's just how things are. You think your feelings are just a box of crayons, and you can pick and choose only the ones you want? Everything is connected. It's like I told you that very first night you were here—nature is everything and its opposite . . ."

". . . and you can't have light without dark," Lucy said slowly, remembering. "You can't have birth without death. You can't have love without heartbreak." She paused. "This is terrible."

Olivia smiled then. "It's the very best part. It makes you completely safe."

"But *life* isn't safe," said Lucy. "It's not supposed to be. I mean, we all *die* in the end!" She found herself shouting now. "And while we're here . . ." But Lucy did not know what she wanted to say. It all seemed so stupid. She wanted . . . what exactly, to be miserable? To feel the loneliness and emptiness she had before?

Lucy felt something happening inside her, a tightening that she almost didn't recognize at first. And then she realized what it was. Longing. Longing for the life she would not, could not, have now.

When there's something you need to know, the universe will keep whispering until you hear it . . .

Lucy gasped and raised her hands to her lips.

And right then, she heard it loud and clear.

She was part of a group of girls who broke hearts on purpose to gain things they wanted. They hurt people and pretended there was something spiritual about it. But they weren't trying to help anyone but themselves.

When she'd joined the Heartbreakers, she'd told herself love made people weak, that it was nothing but a painful trap. But she only thought that because she was going through her own painful heartbreak and could not imagine a way out. The thing is, she didn't have to imagine one—she would have found a way anyway. Time would have passed, and she would have gotten through it all on her own. One day she would have found someone else—a guy at the bookstore reaching for the same book that she was, a guy in her first class on her first day of college, someone walking down the street when she moved to a new city and started her first job. Or maybe she would have been riding around in Tristan's truck one night and turned to the left and finally, finally really seen him. There was no telling what would have happened. And now she'd never know.

Unless . . .

Lucy realized what she wanted as the words left her lips. "I want my old heart back. Is there a way to undo this?"

Olivia's face contorted. Her brow raised and nostrils flared, and her eyes opened wide. It was an expression that Lucy could not place. And it quickly turned to anger. Olivia clenched her jaw. Her voice was cold and hard. "Only an idiot would ever ask that," she said. She got up and walked out of the room without looking back.

Lucy stood in the living room for a long time, unsure of what to do or where to go, hoping beyond reason that Olivia would come back and give her another answer. But it was clear she wasn't going to. Finally Lucy walked back outside, got on her bike, and started the long ride home. She was almost crying. Almost. But the tears wouldn't fall. And she remembered how when she first met Olivia, Olivia had told her, "I don't cry over boys." But Lucy realized what Olivia had really meant: *I don't cry at all.* Heartbreakers never did.

Lucy had always been a crier. Sad things, happy things, touching things, any strong feelings would collect in her eyes and squeeze their way out. Things that would have made her teary included: animals of different species cuddling each other, people cheering while watching their loved ones in a contest, strangers helping each other, weddings and watching other people cry at weddings, people giving hopeful speeches, adults smiling in childlike delight at simple things like when someone handed them an ice-cream cone, pictures of people who have survived hurricanes, pets sitting on the graves of their dead owners. And when anyone at all looked at this messy world that didn't make sense and from the pieces tried to make something beautiful.

Lucy sometimes wondered if being so raw all the time meant she was weak. Now she realized it had nothing to do with that at all. Being open took strength. And being like that was a gift. Life always felt meaningful because she saw meaning in everything.

But all of that was done now. She would never experience any of that ever again. Olivia had said there was no way back, and although Olivia was many things, a liar was not one of them.

Suddenly Lucy stopped her bike right there in the night in the middle of the road, and she gasped. So often we hear what we imagine someone meant instead of what they actually said. When Lucy had asked if there was a way to undo being a Heartbreaker, Olivia had said only an idiot would ask that question.

But she hadn't said no.

Twenty-
Six

♥

For the first time in a long time, Lucy did not see any of the Heartbreakers at school, and there was no talk of their meeting up after. The next day when class was over, Lucy hopped on her bike and rode home all alone. Then she texted Olivia. *Sorry about earlier. I don't know what was wrong with me. What are you up to tonight?*

A few minutes later Olivia texted back: *No worries. No plans yet.*

Lucy smiled. Maybe just maybe, this was going to be easier than she'd thought.

Lucy called Pete. "Hey, Pete," she said. Her voice sounded perfectly calm, but under that cloud of nothing she could feel her pounding heart. "If I tell you something kind of secret, do you swear you'll never tell anyone I told you?"

"Darling, of course. Unless it's terribly good gossip, then I might."

Lucy could hear him grinning.

"I think Olivia's been kind of lonely lately—she'd never admit it, obviously. But I think she could use a night out with someone other than her girlfriends." Lucy imagined Pete at home in his theater, his eyes lighting up, his pulse was quickening. "If you're not busy, do you think you might call her and ask her to do something with you? You know, just come over and watch a movie or something? You have that big projector, right?"

Lucy knew this sounded kind of silly and possibly suspicious. But the truth of the matter is this: People will believe an awful lot of crappy lies if you're suggesting they do what they wanted to do anyway.

"Right, right," Pete said. "Well, I do indeed have that. Hey, cats," Pete called in the background. "Do we have plans tonight?" And then back into the phone he said, "Nope, no plans." She heard a moment of silence, like he was trying to play it cool. "Okay, yeah, we'll call Olivia."

"Thanks, Pete," Lucy said.

Fifteen minutes after that, Lucy texted Olivia again. *Want to go to a movie or something?*

Lucy honestly could not imagine what going to a movie with Olivia alone would even be like. But she wasn't going to find out anytime soon. Thirty seconds later, she received Olivia's response: *Sorry, plans now.*

Lucy smiled. Stage one, complete.

Three hours later, Lucy watched as Pete slowly backed his car down Olivia's driveway. From where she hid, in the bushes across the road, she could see the two of them in the front seat. At the bottom of the driveway, Pete leaned over and kissed Olivia hello, then sped off.

Lucy crossed the street, unlocked the gate, ran up the driveway, and let herself into the house.

She remembered the last time she'd been inside all alone—two months ago, before she was a Heartbreaker, when she was trying to steal magic to use to get Alex back. How long ago it all seemed—it felt like years instead of weeks.

Lucy went up the stairs to Olivia's bedroom and flipped on the light. In the center of the room was an enormous bed, piled high with pillows, covered in green and gold silk. In the middle of the bed was *The Book of Love*. Lucy placed her hand on the cover. "Please, please, please," she whispered, as though that was a spell all of its own.

She heard a slam as someone shut the front door. Then there were footsteps on the stairs.

Crap. Lucy frantically searched for a place to hide.

"Sorry, honey pie," Lucy heard Olivia call from outside the door. "I'll just be a second."

Hands shaking, Lucy flipped off the light and then threw herself into the closet. Lucy peeked through the crack between the door and the jamb and watched as Olivia opened the top drawer of her nightstand. From where she stood, Lucy caught a glimpse of what was inside—a few small potion pots, a couple of vials, and the gold flash of Olivia's tear-catcher necklace. Olivia selected a tiny pot of lotion, opened it up, and rubbed some into her hands, her arms, and her neck. Then she dropped it back in her nightstand and closed the drawer with her hip. Lucy smelled the faint scent of almonds. Empathy Cream.

"Can I come up?" That was Pete now, shouting from the stairs. "I'm coming up, so stop me if you don't want me to!"

Lucy held her breath and backed up farther into the cocoon of Olivia's coats. Her ankle smashed against something in the corner of the closet. Lucy winced and bit her lip.

Through the crack, she saw Pete appear. He wrapped his arms around Olivia's waist and pulled her toward him. Olivia turned and placed her hands on his cheeks. She closed her eyes and stood there for a moment, just holding his face. When Olivia opened her eyes again, her expression had changed. Gone was the veil of detached coolness she always wore. Her face seemed softer now somehow, as though her sharp bones had rounded themselves out. The smile on her lips was small, but real, rich, and warm. Her eyes were twinkling.

And watching her from inside the closet, thinking how very odd it was to see Olivia like that, Lucy suddenly realized she had never seen Olivia happy before right now, not even for a single moment.

But those were not her own feelings changing her face. No, of course, those were Pete's.

And in a flash, it all made perfect sense—why Olivia had put on the Empathy Cream even if there was nothing new she'd find out from wearing it, why her tear-catcher vial wasn't on, and why she'd been aware of Pete's feelings for months, but hadn't yet done anything about them. She hadn't yet because she was never going to. What she wanted was not the power that came from his tears, but the power that came from his love.

Everyone has secrets, Lucy.

"Did you find what you were looking for?" Pete asked.

"Yup," said Olivia. She ran her fingers down his arms, took his hand, and led him back outside.

Lucy counted to one hundred, then reached into the back of the closet, pulled out the thing she'd smashed into, brought it out into the room, and turned on the light.

It was a framed photo of three people sitting on a porch swing. On the left was a man in his early forties, round faced and handsome; on the right was a woman of around the same age, striking with dark hair and bright blue eyes, her etched gold necklace catching the light. And in the middle was a girl, around twelve or thirteen, with her hair pulled back in a ponytail, freckles across her nose, and a tiny space between her two front teeth. The three of them had their arms around each other. They were all laughing.

Lucy stared at the girl in the middle, at her light eyes, sharp cheekbones, dark eyebrows. This was Olivia. And these were her parents.

And judging by the ages of everyone in the picture, this had to have been taken shortly before they died.

How strange it was to see this picture and know what was about to happen. She imagined stepping inside it and warning them, warning this smiling girl who was so different from the Olivia that Lucy now knew.

Lucy shook her head. She put the picture at the back of the closet right where she found it, and she closed the closet door. This wasn't what she was here for. And who knew how long it would take, so she'd better get started.

Twenty-Seven

♥

Hours later Lucy sat slumped on Olivia's floor, *The Book of Love* in front of her. She'd flipped through hundreds of spells, hundreds of recipes for potions and elixirs, hundreds of accounts of hearts broken and tips on how-to, thousands and thousands of pages in total. But there wasn't anything in this book telling her how to rebreak her own heart or even referencing the fact that such a thing was possible. Lucy had thought this was her one chance, but it had never really been a chance at all. Olivia hadn't said no because she didn't have to. Of course there was no going back, there never was. That's not how life worked.

With a freshly broken heart thudding heavy in her chest, Lucy had thought a broken heart was the worst thing in the world. But now Lucy understood that the real worst thing was a completely solid unbreakable one. Lucy breathed out as she stared at that last blank page. This was it for her now. This cold detached feeling was only going to get worse. Worse and worse until it was all she had.

And she realized, then, just how dangerous hope was. The higher it lifted you, the farther you have to fall. And Lucy was falling.

She felt an itch behind her eyes, a strange tingling, a tightening, and finally a release. And for the first time in a very long time, a tear escaped. It dripped out, down her cheek and onto the blank page.

She looked down at the book, blinked twice. Something was happening there now—dark purple words were slowly swirling into view.

Forget the fear, follow the LOV
If you can still cry, it's not too late. . . .

Lucy gasped. Below the words a purple flower with heart-shaped petals was beginning to bloom, green leaves, and vines unfurled below it. And then a moment later the words began to fade, bit by bit, until they, and the flower, were gone.

But it would be burned into her brain forever, that flower, because this wasn't the first time she was seeing it. No. She'd seen it before inked onto skin, lit by fire and moonlight and explosions of sparks.

Now she just needed to find it again.

Twenty-Eight

♥

The next morning, instead of going to school, Lucy rode her bike to the bus station and bought a ticket to Bridgewater. Then she leaned back against the seat and stared out the window, watching the town turn to highway, to trees, to rocks, to hills, to an open field filled with horses, back to trees again, then slowly back to buildings and houses. Two hours after she boarded, the bus stopped at the end of a small town's main street. WELCOME TO BRIDGEWATER, the sign said. And Lucy got off.

"You don't get shows like this in Bridgewater" is what that

girl had said. At the time it had just seemed like the kind of random thing you say to a random stranger who you'll never see again. But now, looking back, Lucy wondered if maybe the girl had been trying to give her a message. Maybe she'd been telling Lucy to come find her. Maybe she had the answers.

Then again, maybe Lucy was just desperate.

She started to walk. Quaint was what people might have called this place, or charming. There was a glass-blowing shop to her right and an ice-cream parlor to her left. And what was Lucy looking for exactly? She had no idea. She just hoped she'd know when she found it.

Lucy passed a used bookstore, a store that sold framed art prints, another that sold organic scented candles, and another filled with fruit-themed baby clothes. She wandered down tiny alleyways and up sets of cobblestone steps. At the top was a pretty little shop with a purple painted awning. LOVELY was written in big white letters, and then below it, SWEET SHOPPE AND CAFÉ. And there was a small sign hanging in the window: TRY OUR HOMEMADE MARSHMALLOWS.

He uses me for my tickets, I use him for his access to treats. That's what Phee had said back at the fire.

In a flash Lucy knew that this was what she'd been looking for.

The door swung open. A woman carrying a small brown bag held the door as she walked out. A wind chime jingled.

Lucy stepped inside.

A dozen or so people sat at tables reading, nibbling snacks, and sipping tea. The shop was filled with purple cushioned chairs set at tiny black wrought-iron tables. Big bold flower paintings hung on the walls. Lucy approached the counter. It was lined with glass cases filled with cookies and sandwiches, and a tower of fluffy white marshmallows.

"Well, hello there," said the girl behind the counter. She had a long dark braid that hung over her shoulder. It was thick like a rope. She was a few years older than Lucy. "Can I help you?"

Lucy looked at the hand-drawn blackboards hung up behind the counter.

"That's our list of organic teas," Braid said.

Lucy's eyes scanned the list: *Peppermint Snow, Orchard Apple, Violet Bloom* . . . And there it was. Next to *Violet Bloom* was a tiny drawing of a flower with heart-shaped petals, curling leaves, and twisted vines.

Lucy's heart was hammering.

"That symbol, next to the violets up there . . ." Lucy pointed.

"You like it?" Braid's lips spread into a smile. "I drew that. Do you want to try the tea? It's pretty delicious."

"No," Lucy said. "I mean, no thank you." Lucy looked at the girl. Did she know? Could she possibly? "Do you happen to know a girl with a tattoo like that?"

Braid tipped her head to the side. "What's her name?"

"I don't know. She has a tattoo of that symbol, though. And I think she lives here, in Bridgewater. She might even work in this café."

Braid shrugged. "Lots of people live here in Bridgewater, and lots of people work here."

"But that flower. Does it mean something? Because I saw it tattooed on a girl's chest and also in a book. . . ."

"What, like a tattoo guide?"

"No," said Lucy. "Like in something . . ." She stopped and took a breath. "Magic."

Braid stared at Lucy like maybe she was crazy.

"Darlin', I have absolutely no idea what you're talking about." She shook her head and motioned to a tray on the counter. "Would you like a free sample of our chocolate marzipan cake? Now *that's* what I call magic."

"No thank you," Lucy said. "I just . . ."

Lucy was watching Braid's face, trying to figure out what to say next, and then something happened: Braid's eyes flicked down to Lucy's chest and focused on her tattoo. A tattoo she should not have been able to see.

Lucy looked back up. Their eyes met. The girl reached up to her own chest, as if on instinct. And through the sheer fabric of her floaty white shirt, Lucy saw the outline of a deep purple flower.

"I'm not one of them anymore," Lucy said quickly. "Or at least I don't want to be."

"One of who?"

"The Secret Sisterhood of Heartbreakers," said Lucy. "That's why I came here. I'm trying to find my way out. . . ."

Braid's expression turned serious. She placed her own hand over her tattoo. "Put your hand on your heart," Braid said. And Lucy did. Then Braid reached out and took Lucy's hand. And she stood there for a minute with her eyes closed, just breathing. Lucy felt something shoot up her arm, and then there was a tingling in her chest. Braid opened her eyes and she nodded.

"Well, why didn't you say that in the first place?" the girl said. She smiled. "I'm Clara. Follow me."

Twenty-Nine

♥

They walked for a long time, mostly in silence. And as they did, Lucy realized that if this girl was indeed magic too, then her magic was different from Lucy's. She watched the way Clara seemed to engage with absolutely everything and everyone around her—she waved at an older couple holding hands, smiled at a father holding a newborn baby, and when a dog ran by and dropped its slobbery rubber toy at her feet, Clara picked it up and threw it hard. She wasn't separated from this world, she was a part of all of it.

Finally they reached a white stone house with huge

plate-glass windows. The walkway leading up to it was lined with brightly colored enamel pots. Growing out of each was a bunch of violets.

"Here we are," Clara said.

They made their way to the front door. It opened before they knocked. And there was the girl from SoundWave. She was grinning. "Hey, stranger," she said. "Well, this is a surprise." But she didn't look surprised at all.

"See you later, chickies," Clara said. She waved to both of them. "I better get back before the locals take off with all the cheese sandwiches."

"Bunch of ruffians around here," said SoundWave girl. And both of them laughed.

Then she swung the door open and stepped aside. "Come in. I'm Kai, by the way."

"I'm—" said Lucy.

"Lucy." Kai nodded. "I know."

Kai led Lucy into an enormous high-ceilinged living room that connected to an open kitchen. There was a massive sectional sofa in the center of the room on a fluffy white rug facing a glass and white stone fireplace. Above the mantel was a huge painting of a warrior goddess done in reds and browns and golds. Through the windows at the back was a large deck overlooking a garden, a greenhouse, and a little stream.

There were at least twenty women there, maybe more.

They were of all different ages, from around Lucy's age all the way up to the two women chatting at the kitchen counter, who appeared to be in their seventies or eighties. Some of the women were typing on sleek-looking laptops, two were painting, a few were relaxing with books.

"Lucy, this is everyone," Kai said. The girls and women looked up and smiled. They looked friendly and artsy and smart, like they all probably read a lot of books and volunteered at animal shelters and made their own stained glass or ran a literary magazine. "Guys," said Kai. "This is Lucy. The one I told you about."

"You told them about me?"

Kai nodded. "I thought you might try to find us."

"You did?"

"When we watched the fireworks together, I just . . . had a feeling."

"So it wasn't random coincidence that you were at SoundWave, was it?"

Kai shook her head. "We knew Beacon Drew was on the HHB's list." Lucy's eyebrows shot up at the mention. Kai smiled at Lucy's surprise. "The Heartbreakers are a powerful bunch, but we have a few tricks of our own. We knew the concert would be filled with Heartbreakers. And where there are Heartbreakers, there are the heartbroken. And the people who need us tend to find us. I guess this time, that was you."

"Who are you?" said Lucy.

"We're the League of Violets. But some people just call us the LOVs."

"And . . . what are you? Are you connected to the Heartbreakers somehow?"

Kai shook her head again. "We're just people who've had our hearts broken."

"Are you . . ."—it sounded so silly to say—"magic?"

"Let's put it this way: We know how to access certain forces that most people do not. But we don't do it very often. We like life the way it is."

"And what do you all *do*?"

"We have fun, we make art, we fall in love." She pointed to the tattoo on her chest. "Our symbol is the violet. Every night they close up, but when morning comes, violets open and point themselves toward the light. Every morning, again and again, no matter how dark the darkness was."

"That's . . ." She wanted to say *really beautiful*, but the words sounded too stupid in her head, so she was silent.

"And if we happen to meet someone who needs us to remind them that that choice exists for them too, we do it."

Lucy nodded.

Kai smiled. "So now we've told you who we are," she said. "Who are you?"

"What do you want to know?"

"How about you start at the beginning," Kai said.

So Lucy did. "Less than two months ago, I had my heart

broken and I thought it was the worst moment of my life." Lucy looked down. "I was wrong about that." And she went on. She told them about Alex, about Tristan, about meeting Olivia, about completing their Heartbreaker family. She told them about her parents, about the Breakies and *The Book of Love*. About not being able to cry at all and then finally crying and seeing that violet blooming there as though her tear had made the flower grow. She told them how very, very badly she knew she wanted her heart back, even though every moment she could feel that less and less.

When Lucy was done, Kai smiled as though nothing Lucy had said or could say would ever shock her. She motioned to a spot on the couch. Lucy let herself sink into it. Kai walked away, and when she returned a moment later, she was holding a violet silk drawstring satchel.

"We will try to help you the best we can," said Kai. "But there's good news and bad news."

From the satchel she removed a piece of carved amethyst. "This is the mold for what is known as a Rebreaking Blade." She held it out. "It's hollow, but if a powerful Heartbreaker fills it with brokenhearted tears and pulls up energy from the center of the earth, a blade will form inside it. Then the mold is smashed away, and what's left is a blade made of tears, pain solidified. It is the only thing strong enough to get through the impenetrable wall of an unbreakable heart."

"So what does that mean? How does it work?"

Kai took a breath. "You have to stab yourself in the heart."

"Is it . . ." Lucy knew it was a stupid question as she heard the words come out of her mouth. "Safe?"

Kai looked down. "No. Not even when it works exactly as it's supposed to." When she looked back up, all trace of a smile was gone from her lips. "When it works perfectly, all the feelings you avoided by having an unbreakable heart come back to you and demand to be felt, all at once. That means the heartbreak you were escaping in the first place, and everything else that happened to you in the time your heart wasn't working, and all the guilt over all the hearts you broke. But it's not just that. You also have to feel the pain of all the boys who cried the tears that make up your blade. When the blade enters your heart, you absorb whatever was left of their heartbreaks, and their hearts heal back."

"Wow," said Lucy. "That's . . ."

Kai nodded. "The grief drives people crazy sometimes. But that's only if you get the chance to feel it, which is the very best case. In order for it to work at all, your heart has to be filled with enough love to deflect the blade and keep it from . . ." Kai trailed off.

"To keep it from what?"

"If your heart is empty, then the blade will affect it like any regular blade would." Her voice was only a whisper now. "Which means . . ."

Lucy looked up. She felt all the blood drain from her face,

and a prickle of terror poked through her impenetrable heart. Kai didn't have to finish because Lucy understood perfectly. Getting an unbreakable heart had ended her life. Getting her old heart back could kill her.

"It's why we never just outright offer the blade to Heartbreakers—they have to really want it, they have to come and find us."

Lucy's entire body was tingling. The room was silent. "Okay," said Lucy slowly. She took a breath. "So then what's the good news?"

Kai sucked air in through her teeth. "That was the good news. The bad news is that only an incredibly powerful Heartbreaker can make the blade. How many hearts have you broken?"

"Two," Lucy said. "The one I broke to join, and one other."

Kai looked for a moment very sad and very sorry. "Then you're not powerful enough yet."

"And you can't make it for me, I'm guessing," Lucy said.

"I wish we could."

"So how many do I have to break to make it?" Lucy felt her face grow hot.

"A hundred."

"You're joking." Lucy's words hung in the air. "Even Olivia hasn't broken that many."

But of course, Kai wasn't joking at all. And there was nothing to say beyond that. Lucy knew she'd never get to a hundred hearts. Even if she had the skill for it, she didn't have the stomach. All those boys brokenhearted. For what? So she could undo her own terrible mistake?

"I don't know what to say," Lucy said.

"I'm really sorry," Kai said. "I'm sorry it isn't easier than this."

Lucy was too numb to feel the crushing disappointment that she knew was just behind that wall surrounding her heart.

What would she do now? How would she live the rest of her life like this?

In the kitchen, someone stood. She was watching Lucy as she started walking toward her. When their eyes met, Lucy felt a flash of recognition. But who was she?

The woman had thick white hair, ice-blue eyes, and high-sculpted cheekbones. She was wearing a flowing sapphire top and loose black silk pants. A huge amber necklace hung from her neck, and she had a ring on every finger. She was tall and held herself like a queen. Lucy realized where she'd seen her before.

"I think we know someone in common," Lucy said.

She stared at the face of the woman in front of her. She'd seen this woman in black and white, forty years younger in a portrait in Olivia's living room. She'd been in this woman's closet, worn this woman's clothes, heard stories about her, and read her very own words written in *The Book of Love*.

This was Eleanor de Lune, Olivia's grandmother. Olivia's grandmother who was supposed to be dead.

"Yes," Eleanor said coolly. "I believe that we do."

"You're . . . ," Lucy whispered.

"Alive?" said Eleanor. She arched one dark eyebrow, just the way Olivia would have. "Apparently."

"Does she know?"

Eleanor nodded. Then stood there, silently. She looked like she was making a decision. "May I?" she said to Kai. Kai nodded. Eleanor took the Rebreaking Blade mold and slipped it in her big straw tote. She held out her hand to Lucy. "Come with me," she said. "I need to show you something."

Lucy hugged Kai and bid her good-byes to this warm house, to the girls and women inside it.

"You're welcome here anytime," Kai said.

But Lucy knew she would not be back.

Thirty

♥

Lucy followed Eleanor out the door, around a corner, and up to a small yellow house with an apple tree in the front yard. Eleanor led her inside into its cozy living room. There was an enormous bouquet of sunset-colored flowers on a light wooden table, an eggplant-colored couch sat behind it, and underneath was a slightly worn Native American–looking rug laid out on the polished wood floors. Quiet music was playing in the background, pan flutes mixed with the sounds of the ocean.

Through one window, Lucy spotted a small backyard, where an older gentleman was sitting at a table, two giant black dogs curled up at his feet. Eleanor waved at him. He blew her a kiss. Then Eleanor motioned for Lucy to sit.

"I have a couple of things to give you, if you don't mind."

Lucy nodded.

Eleanor walked to a roll-top desk, opened the drawer, and took out a thick stack of letters. *RETURN TO SENDER* was written on the back of each in Olivia's slanted script. Eleanor took one off the top. "I've been trying to get a letter to my granddaughter for two and a half years. Maybe you'll have better luck. Read it yourself if you want." She handed the envelope to Lucy.

Then Eleanor reached up and removed a necklace, a small one that had been hidden behind the amber. She held up a thin gold chain from which dangled an intricately carved locket. "I've been saving this for her too." Eleanor took Lucy's hand and lowered the locket down into it. The metal was warm. Lucy stared at it. It looked familiar, and Lucy realized why she recognized it. She'd seen it in the photo in the back of Olivia's closet.

"The hospital gave it to me after my daughter died," Eleanor said. "Olivia should have it. Her mother would have wanted her to." There were tears in Eleanor's eyes. "Go ahead, look inside."

Lucy pried the halves apart. In one side there was a photograph of a woman cradling a baby, gazing at the baby with a look of pure love. In the other half of the locket there was a tiny violet behind glass. "The woman is my daughter, and the baby is Olivia, of course. I don't know where the violet came from. My daughter wasn't a Heartbreaker and would never have known of the LOVs. It's probably just a coincidence. Or maybe"—Eleanor smiled—"it's just a bit of magic." She paused. "But that isn't why I brought you here." She went back to the roll-top desk, and from the top drawer she removed a small silver box. "This is," she said. She handed it to Lucy. "Open it."

Lucy lifted the lid and stared down at a pile of withered purple petals.

"Those are enchanted violets," said Eleanor. "I made them a very long time ago, back when I was still a Heartbreaker and still had the power to make such things. I made them for Olivia in case she ever wanted them. But the more time that passes, the less hope I have that she'll ever want them. And the right thing to do is to give them to someone who will actually use them, instead of save them for someone who probably never will. When you're ready, brew them into a tea and drink."

"And then what?"

"Then you'll be powerful enough to make the blade, without having to break any more hearts. You'll still need to somehow find the tears to fill the mold with, but you'll at least be capable of crafting it when you have them."

"I . . . ," Lucy started to say. She stared down at the tiny silver box. She wanted to thank her, but it was all too much.

"I don't even know how to . . ."

"You don't need to." Eleanor took Lucy's hand in hers. "I turned Olivia into a Heartbreaker, and she turned you into one. You could say I owe you this." Eleanor took a deep breath and looked Lucy right in the eye. "But be careful. The violets will make you more powerful than any person should ever be. Make your peace with this world before you drink the tea because once you do, you might not come back."

Then she took Lucy's shoulders and pulled her in for a hug.

"If you . . ." She stopped. "If this goes okay, maybe you'll come by and visit me sometime? Tell me how my granddaughter is doing?"

Lucy nodded. "I promise I will."

The door to the backyard opened and the man from outside walked in, the two dogs circling his feet.

"Hope I'm not interrupting," he said.

Eleanor quickly wiped her eyes and she smiled. "No, of course not," she said. "Lucy, this is Harry. Harry, honey, this is Lucy."

Harry smiled and tipped his hat. "Well, it's a pleasure to meet you." He held out his hand and shook Lucy's. Then leaned down and kissed Eleanor on the cheek. Eleanor flushed and turned toward Harry. Their eyes met. And Lucy did not need any kind of potion to see just what this was.

Thirty-One

♥

The bus bounced along, and Lucy flicked on the overhead light. She took the letter off her lap, opened the flap, and pulled out four sheets of creamy white paper. The handwriting was elegant and bold. She began to read.

Dear Olivia,

I know that after what I've done, I don't deserve to have you in my life. And I know that you will probably return this letter unopened as you've done with all the others, but I have told you so many lies over the years, and you deserve to understand the choice I made for you and the one you are continuing to make. You deserve to know the truth.

So here it is, my story right from the beginning, starting back when I was just an innocent naive girl with a soft heart that had not yet been broken. And unlike the stories I told you in person, this one is true.

It was Christmas Eve of my seventeenth year when I got my first kiss. His name was Albert, and he was twenty. I'd loved him from afar for years, but only recently had he noticed me at all. We were standing together under a frozen starry sky when he handed me a small box covered in gold paper and tied with a satin bow. I saw the care with which the box had been wrapped, and I knew this meant he loved me too. That realization was the happiest moment of my life up until that point. Funny how we can "know" things that turn out not to be true at all. Our brains are liars, and sometimes so are our hearts. But I hadn't learned that, not yet.

I forced myself to unwrap it slowly, imagining what might be inside—a silk scarf to match my eyes, a book of love poems, maybe a bracelet or pin that I'd wear every day so I would always have him with me. I held my breath as I opened the box, cheeks sore from smiling. And there it was, his gift to me: a clump of dirt and a small dead bug. I could barely believe what I was seeing.

It was a joke, of course. It was supposed to be funny. Albert certainly thought it was. "But you said you'd love whatever I got you!" he said. I tried to laugh, but my lip was quivering. And this made Albert just laugh harder. And when he was finally done laughing, he turned my face toward his, and that was when he kissed me for the very first time.

Two months later, we were married. And a few weeks after that, he went off to fight in the war. I was sick with missing him. I wrote him every day, and dreamed of him every night. He didn't write back, but I told myself that was because he was far away, fighting, scared for his life. Three months after he left, I got my first letter. The envelope was thin, the handwriting on the back dark and neat. My first thought was that it was a letter from his lieutenant telling me my Albert had died. Instead, what was inside that envelope shook me almost as much as that news would have. It was a single paragraph from Albert, in which he told me he had fallen in love with another girl, that I should get in touch with someone his father knew who could take care of the divorce. There was only one other thing in the envelope, a ribbon I had sent with him, my best hair ribbon, which I thought might bring him luck. Perhaps he thought that it had.

I was as devastated as one might expect. That first night, I sat there sobbing for hours, staring at a picture from our wedding, the only picture I had of the two of us. But the next day, my aunt Esther came to see me, all billowing scarves and exotic perfume. "Ellie, baby," she said. "If you do what I say, I can fix your heart." I did not question for a single moment whether listening to her was the right thing to do. And when she told me to break a heart, I did not hesitate, as there'd been a neighborhood fellow in love with me all his life. I became a Heartbreaker then. It was years before I ever looked back.

I left home not long after that with a few dollars and Esther's going-away presents—a sack of potions, and a small book containing the names and addresses of a dozen other Heartbreakers. It turned out to be more than enough.

Years passed and life went on. And some of what I told you happened during that time actually did. When the war ended, I traveled the world. I got married a few times, sometimes for money, sometimes for amusement. I married a prince, then an artist, then a diplomat. I never had a Heartbreaker family—Aunt Esther had not made me part of hers—and I never recruited any others. And because of that, my power grew slowly and the barrier around my heart grew slowly too. I barely even realized that every time I broke a heart, or used magic for anything, the shell got a tiny bit thicker. The same is happening to you. I wonder if you've noticed yet.

When she was dying, Aunt Esther summoned me to her bedside. And I remember so distinctly exactly what she said. "People think memory is stored in the brain. But everything that truly matters is stored in the heart. If your heart is locked shut, your life won't mean anything." She told me she'd wasted her life by spending it as a Heartbreaker, and if I didn't find a way out, I'd waste mine too. She also told me she'd heard that there was a way out, that there was a group who maybe could help. I just needed to go find them.

I didn't listen to her then. I decided she was a crazy old woman, and if she was full of regrets, it was only because she hadn't really lived. Not the way I was! Look at all the places I'd been! At all the people I'd met! At the fortune I had! Of course, I didn't really care about any of it, but that, I thought, was beside the point.

It wasn't long after that that I got pregnant with your mother. It was an accident, of course. Her father, your grandfather, was a sweet musician who loved me. I didn't even realize I was going to have a baby until I'd already left him with a broken heart. When she was born, I brought her to her father, who I hadn't seen in months. I watched the way his eyes immediately changed when he gazed at his child, who he hadn't even known existed five minutes before. There was such caring and deep love there. I found it equal parts confusing and pathetic. I left her with him. And I was free again. I thought that was what I wanted.

By that point, my life was entirely empty. It had been years since I'd had any sort of connection with anyone. I told myself I did not care. That I wanted it that way. But I was *too numb to have any idea of what I might have wanted.*

I visited your mother occasionally at first, then less and less often as time went on. When you were born, I was in Paris, and I remember her telling me over the phone that she would be the mother to you that I had never been to her. And I told her good luck, but thought what a fool she was even to want to try.

Then something happened: the accident. And I don't need to tell you about that. I was your closest living relative, so you came to stay with me despite—and I am ashamed to say this, but it's true and I'm trying to tell the truth here—my best attempts to find somewhere else for you to go. It was a week before your thirteenth birthday. And when you arrived at my house, with nothing but a suitcase bigger than you were, and a bewildered look on your face, I actually felt something for the first time in longer than I could recall. I thought, "This is not a pain this child should have to deal with." And so I found a way to make you one of us. You were the blood descendant of a Heartbreaker, which meant I could easily give you what I thought was a valuable and remarkable gift—the gift of an impenetrable, unbreakable heart. And you know what happened next—I taught you how to win a boy and how to break him.

And just like that, you were okay.

You never had to grieve for your mother and father. You never could.

But you still needed someone to learn from, so I taught you what I knew, or what I thought I knew anyway. You loved my stories—you insisted I tell you all about my life. And I didn't mind. I liked seeing someone else's reaction to my life, because while living it, I had barely felt anything at all. And I suppose this is the crux of what I am trying to say: I told you stories the way I knew you wanted to hear them, the way I wished they went, instead of how they actually happened. When the Venezuelan poet took me to that waterfall, I did not stand in awe of the beauty and the power of that rushing water. When the Parisian composer dedicated a symphony to me, there were no tears in my eyes.

Appreciating art, music, poetry—that requires an open heart, which I did not have. And when you came to live with me and told me you loved me, and I said "I love you" back, I never really did, never could until now.

By the time you were fourteen, I felt nothing but the occasional buzz of power, and a boring, listless emptiness. And that's when I realized that Esther had been right all along— I had wasted my life. And it was my fault that you were wasting yours too. So I told you my very last lie—that I was dying, and that I was leaving to do it in peace. It seemed easier than telling you the truth and taking the risk that you'd try to stop me, or come with. And I left and went in search of a way back. I vowed to find it or die trying.

And I suppose that was my last in a series of unforgivable mistakes—not giving you the chance to follow me when you might have. I am so sorry I didn't.

I know I have no right to suppose what your mother may have wanted, but one thing I do know for sure, she wouldn't want you to spend your time on this planet like this. She would want you to live, to love.

Please come see me and let me help to make this right.

Love always,

Your grandmother

Hours later, Lucy got off the bus and pedaled home to an empty house. She walked slowly from room to room. It was cleaner than she'd ever seen it before. Everything was put away. The kitchen was spotless, and there was a big vase of flowers on the counter. It was all fresh and brand-new. She went upstairs to her parents' room and opened her father's dresser. There was nothing there but a single navy blue sock.

So they were really doing it this time.

Lucy took out her phone and dialed Gil.

"What's up, slut?" Gil said. Her tone was light and easy.

"When I was at your house before, you said you'd teach me how to open the safe. I want to know now. Can you tell me how to do it?"

"I'M ON THE PHONE WITH HER RIGHT NOW, LIZA!" Gil yelled into the background. And then back into the phone she said, "There's some house party on Darby

Street tonight. Hot guys, strong drinks. We're going around ten. You in?"

Lucy stared at her phone. *Huh?* "No," she said. "No, I don't think so. But about the safe . . ."

"Well, suit yourself," Gil said, and then she hung up. Lucy stood there. She had no idea what had just happened.

But a few minutes later the phone rang. "Listen," Gil whispered. "Here's what you need to do. . . ."

Thirty-Two

The driveway was empty when Lucy arrived. She dropped her bike on the grass and slipped inside the house. Lucy knew they must have just left—the scent of perfume, amber, and musk still hung in the air. Lucy went up to the magic room, flipped on the lights, and pulled up the floorboard, revealing the dark gray safe. She took two bobby pins from her pocket, bent them into Ls, and then, hands shaking slightly, inserted them into the keyhole, just the way Gil had told her to. She twisted carefully, listened for the clicks, and pulled one pin back and pushed the other forward. She held her breath and gave one final tweak, and the lock popped. She opened the door to the safe, and there in front of her were piles and piles of tiny amber vials. Each contained the tear of a brokenhearted boy.

Lucy reached out and grabbed a handful and tossed them into her backpack. She grabbed another, and another until the safe was empty. She closed the door, locked the lock, and put the floorboard back.

Then she walked into Olivia's room, placed Eleanor's letter on her pillow, and draped the locket next to it.

She headed for the door. She could hear the tiny glass vials clattering in her backpack. She rode home.

She went upstairs and got into bed and lay there, silent and still, brain racing, body on fire. She lay like that, wide-awake until morning.

Thirty-Three

♥

Before she left for school, Lucy hugged her mother good-bye. "I hope you have an okay day, Mom" was what Lucy said. But what she was thinking was *If this doesn't work, I am so, so sorry.* Her mother smiled vaguely. "I'll be okay, honey," she said. "I feel better than I have in a very long time."

Lucy made her way through the day, and she wondered why she had even bothered to go to school at all. Maybe she just wanted to see it all—her school, her teachers, all those people who'd made up her days and been somehow a part of her life—and say good-bye, just in case. Then again, maybe she'd just wanted to see Tristan.

Olivia hadn't come to school again. Neither had Liza. Lucy saw Gil in the hallway, wild-eyed, standing alone. She spotted Jason and Jessica in the parking lot, holding hands, laughing. But there was no sign of Tristan's lanky frame, his floppy hair, his smiling eyes. Which meant the last time she saw him might have actually been the very last.

At the end of the day, Lucy got a cup of hot water from the cafeteria and then sprinkled in the tiny handful of petals. She waited until the water turned faintly purple, and then she took a sip. It tasted like perfume. Her tongue began to tingle, and her throat numbed as the liquid went down. She felt her insides lurch, like the room was an elevator going down. Everything around her went quiet. And then Lucy felt her mouth spreading into a smile.

Sometimes the truth reveals itself slowly, like a flower gently blooming. Other times it will hit you like a punch in the gut, so hard and fast you'll be lucky to catch your breath.

Dizzy, gasping, giddy, Lucy packed up her things and stumbled toward the bathroom. Her body was buzzing with energy so intense she felt like she was about to fly right out of her own skin.

The truth that had revealed itself was this: She was young

and beautiful and powerful and free. *And there was no way in hell she was ever giving that up.*

She pushed into the empty bathroom and locked the door behind her. She closed her eyes and felt the blood zipping through her veins, felt her gorgeous heart steel strong at the center of herself. She felt power shooting up from the center of the earth, up through her feet and legs, filling her entire body. She forced herself to breathe. And when her heart slowed ever so slightly, she opened her eyes and stared at herself in the cracked glass.

She was absolutely stunning. A stunning, amazing, luminous creature. She'd gotten some sun at SoundWave, and her skin was the color of honey. Her hair hung down, shiny and white, and without her rock chick blowout it lay in soft loose waves. She looked like a surfer chick about to hit the beach, like someone who didn't have a care in the world.

How ridiculous that she'd spent the last seven weeks *worrying* about things. About everything! She'd worried about not hurting Colin's feelings, about helping Tristan, even about getting back to the boring way she used to be. *When all along, she should have been having fun.*

She looked at her phone. It was three thirty on a Tuesday. And that meant only one thing: time to party.

Lucy wasn't going to call her sisters, not this time. She didn't want anything to do with Gil, who was a liar, and Liza, who was a mess. And Olivia, well, who knew what Olivia was. And who even cared. Lucy had almost sacrificed this amazing gift simply because she didn't like what and who surrounded it. Well, that made no sense. She could throw them out so easily. She already had.

She was more powerful than any of them now, all on her own.

Of course, she didn't have to stay on her own. She started scrolling through her phone. There were so many guys' numbers in there now, all but one from just the last seven weeks. Adam S, Adam T, Brian, Colin, Darien, Dex, Diego H. The list went on and on. She closed her eyes as she tried to picture their faces. Problem was, she barely remembered meeting most of them. Many of them were guys her sisters knew, a few she'd met out at parties and such. None of them were people she knew *intimately*. But now there was time for that. . . .

She hovered over a name: *Hotness*. Who the hell was *Hotness*? She had no idea. But she was about to find out.

Lucy reached in her bag, pulled out a crushed cherry gloss, and slicked it on. Then she used her phone to record a little video of her lips blowing a kiss at the screen.

She played it back. In the video her lips were all you could see. She looked luscious, sexy, and completely mysterious. She wrote, *Plans this afternoon?* And then with no hesitation at all, she hit SEND. She took a breath and started to count.

One broken heart, two broken hearts, three broken hearts . . .

By the time she got to ten, he'd written her back.

Meet me at Merchant Park in twenty minutes?

Lucy smirked. *Make it fifteen.*

Thirty-Four

♥

When their eyes met, she let her lips curl into a smile. Hotness held her gaze, then held up one finger, and beckoned, as though she would do what he told her to.

Well, he could think that. For now . . .

She leaned her bike up against a lamppost, then started walking toward him, letting her hips sway. She could feel him watching her as she realized two things: One, she had absolutely no idea who this guy was, and two, his name was a serious understatement.

Hotness wasn't simply hot. He was smoldering. He was

tall, easily six foot three, and strong-looking. He had huge hands, sparkly eyes, and a sexy mean-looking mouth. There was energy coming off him; she could feel that from fifteen feet away, something pure and raw. He looked like he was in his late teens, or even early twenties.

This was going to be more fun than she'd thought.

"So," Hotness said. His voice was low. "I've seen your lips, now let's get a good look at the rest of you." He gave her the slow up-and-down, lingering on her bare legs, then her mouth. His eyes were teardrop blue. "I knew lips like that had to be connected to something good. Now, who the hell are you?"

Lucy started to laugh. "So you don't know me either?"

But Hotness wasn't laughing. "Either?"

Lucy shrugged. "I just picked your number randomly out of my phone, I don't even know how I got it."

He raised one eyebrow. "You have good timing there, sweetheart. Your message was kind of impossible to resist."

He reached into his pocket then and pulled out a pack of cigarettes. He placed one between his lips and lit it. The blue smoke curled up. Usually Lucy hated the smell of cigarettes, but in that moment it was completely delicious, harsh and sharp and real.

And then suddenly Lucy remembered how she'd gotten Hotness's number: Six weeks ago when Lucy was just a brand-new baby Heartbreaker, her sisters had taken her to a party at Jack and B's. They'd all been on the steps out front, and Hotness had been smoking, which Lucy remembered because the smoke had made her cough, and she was worried it sounded gross. Liza was sloppy drunk that night. She'd dropped her own phone into the toilet and had demanded Lucy hand hers over. Then she'd fished Hotness's phone out of his pocket, called Lucy on it, and stored the number, without even asking him. Hotness had just stood there, smoking his cigarette, shaking his head. It was the first time Lucy had ever seen Liza chase a boy, and the only time, apart from the debacle with Beacon, that it hadn't worked. "He'll be glad when I call him," Liza kept slurring, for the rest of the night. "He was just trying to play it coooool."

But the next morning Liza had forgotten about him, or at least sobered up enough and decided to pretend to. And Lucy had forgotten about him as well. Until now.

"So," Lucy said. "Now that we're both here, what are we going to do this afternoon?"

"Maybe we should buy some lottery tickets," said Hotness. "Because I can already tell you're a very lucky girl."

"Oh?" Lucy said. She arched her back slightly and looked down at her body as though to imply it was a product of her luck. Then smirked slightly. "To what specific aspect of my luck are you referring?"

"To your very lucky timing," he said. And he took a step forward. "Because if you'd sent that video an hour from now, you'd have missed me completely. I'd already be gone." He pointed through the window to the back of the car. There was a big black duffel bag on the seat.

"Heading on a vacation?"

"More like I'm leaving."

"Why's that?"

Hotness twisted his lips into a smirk. "If you really want to know, I broke a heart."

"Naughty boy," Lucy said. "Whose?"

Hotness looked kind of proud. "My girlfriend's. We were living together. So now it's time to go."

"And where are you headed?"

Hotness shrugged. "I don't know," he said. "L.A. maybe? Austin? Miami? Seattle? Mexico? The future is wide-open."

Lucy closed her eyes. She tried to imagine herself in all of those other places. And suddenly she realized something— she could go if she wanted. She could leave forever. No one could stop her.

"And you're going by yourself?"

"That was the plan," he said.

"That's too bad," said Lucy. "I think we could have had some"—she raised her eyebrows—"fun together."

"Well . . . ," he said slowly. "I could probably be convinced to take a hitchhiker with me. Know anyone who might be up for an adventure?"

Lucy paused. She was floating far away. She wondered what

she was going to do. *What's Lucy doing now?* she thought, like she was some other person. The surge of power she'd felt when she drank the violets was flickering. If it went out, she'd be plunged into darkness.

And just like that, the decision was made.

"Well, when do we leave?" Lucy said.

Hotness's face spread into a hesitant smile, like he wasn't quite sure what was happening. "Seriously? Aren't you scared, going off on your own with a guy you don't even know?"

"What do I have to be scared of?" She felt the world shift under her feet. "I'm magic."

"Oh yeah?" said Hotness. He was fully grinning now. "How's that?"

"I break boys' hearts," she said. "And I use their tears to perform magic." She could say anything; she could do anything. There were no rules at all anymore. "I am powerful beyond anything you could ever imagine."

"Is that right?" Hotness wasn't smiling quite as wide anymore. "So what are you, like a witch or something?"

"Not exactly," Lucy said. Her voice was smooth and low. "Then again, not exactly not."

"Well, not-exactly-witch woman . . ." Hotness blew smoke out of the corner of his mouth, then tossed his cigarette onto the pavement. "Are you going to cast a spell on me?" He started to lean in.

"Maybe I already have."

He moved in closer. She felt his breath on her face. She closed her eyes for a single split second. A face flashed in her mind. This—right here, right now, this kiss with this guy—was not what she wanted. *It was so, so far from anything she ever had wanted.*

She pushed Hotness away. His eyes popped open.

"Actually . . . ," she said. Her voice was shaking now. She was very cold. Something was happening. Inside her some part of her was trying to get out. "I don't think this is a very good idea."

Hotness laughed. "Well, of course it isn't a good idea, but why the hell would that stop us from doing it?"

"You need to leave, leave now before I make a terrible choice worse than I've already done."

He snorted. "You're a freak, you know that?" Hotness gave her a last look, a final up-and-down. "Too bad. You hot ones are always insane."

He got into his car. His tires screeched as he drove away.

Lucy looked around her—at the empty parking lot, the sky, the sun, his cigarette butt on the asphalt, still curling up smoke. She felt the violets buzzing inside her. What the hell was she *doing*?

She was floating through space, tethered to nothing. She was going to float away. She could feel it happening. She'd be lost forever. She needed something or someone to bring her back.

Tristan. She pictured his sweet face, his squinty blue eyes, the way he looked when he said good-bye.

She could call him and ask him to play her a song on his harmonica, the way he always used to when she was upset. He would bring her home. She reached for her phone. She scrolled to his number. She was about to dial.

She stopped, finger frozen in the air.

Tristan had said he couldn't be friends with her right now. And she had to respect that. He deserved at least that much. But it wasn't just that.

All along she'd been looking for someone else to make it okay, to make her okay, Alex, Tristan, the Heartbreakers. Only in that moment, she finally understood something: If she needed a song to save her, she could make her own.

Thirty-Five

♥

"A rt Cavanaugh, Jesse Quartermaine, Sebastian Clark." As she unpacked each vial, Lucy whispered the name printed on the side. "Mark Colby, Mark Rutherford, Mark Durante." One by one she laid them out in front of her. "Hector Dean, Zachary Hynde, Ben Gordon." She kept going until her backpack was empty and there were 103 vials on her bed—103 boys who'd had their hearts needlessly broken.

Lucy wondered where each of them was now. Who had let go and moved on? Who was still waiting for a phone call that would never come?

She pinched a vial between her fingers. *Andres Pink.* "Thank you," she whispered, "and I hope I can help." She unscrewed the top and upended the vial over her measuring cup. A single drop dribbled out. She put the empty vial aside and reached for the next one, and the next one. She did this with each vial, whispering the same thing each time, until they were all empty and there was a little pond of tears at the bottom of the glass.

She held up the cup and tipped the tears into the base of the mold. Then she closed her eyes. She concentrated on channeling the energy up from the center of the earth, out through her hands as she squeezed that cold smooth stone. She took a breath and felt a flood of relief as the power from the enchanted violets left her body.

It meant the blade was ready.

And then, only then, did she allow herself to finally really face what she was about to do: *She was going to stab herself in the heart.*

The thought made her sick with a fear so deep even her Heartbreaker heart could feel it. But there was no other choice; there was no other option. That Lucy knew for sure.

Because it wasn't just about her anymore. No. It was about everyone she'd come across for the entire rest of her life, and the ripples she would spread.

If she didn't do what she needed to do, her Heartbreaker

heart would just get harder and harder. And no matter what vows she might make now—to only use her magic for good, to never hurt anyone on purpose—it was useless to pretend she was in a position to make promises. The Lucy who made these vows wouldn't exist as soon as one of her sisters broke another heart. She couldn't trust herself not to change her mind. And then what? She would stop caring about the state of anyone else's heart. She would spread pain wherever she went and convince herself it was okay. And there were too many people like that already. The world did not need any more.

Lucy walked down the stairs quietly in the dark. She went into the backyard and laid the amethyst out on a rock. Then she lifted a large heavy stone and brought it down, smashing the purple casing to pieces, revealing what was underneath. She took a breath. There right in front of her, shimmering and swirling, was a blade made of tears. Lucy touched the tip with her finger and watched a bead of blood rise up like a jewel. It was ready, it was time. And she could not lose her nerve.

She held the blade in two fists, then pointed it toward the smooth skin of her breastbone.

She gave herself a countdown.

Five.

Four.

Three.

Two.

But at the last second Lucy froze. If she really wanted to make things right, she couldn't do this. Not yet. There was still one more thing she needed to do.

Thirty-Six

♥

There was a tangle of drunk people on the steps. Someone tried to give Lucy a plastic cup. Someone else tried to grab her hand and get her to dance. Lucy barely even saw them. She pushed past into the party.

"Hey, Lucicle," a voice said. There was Jack. He had his arm around a girl who looked like a female version of him. "I heard you weren't coming out tonight."

"I'm on a mission," Lucy said. She tried to smile. "Have you seen my friends?"

He pointed toward the back of the house. "Follow the trail

of brokenhearted boys," he said with a grin. But really he had no idea how right he was.

Lucy made her way forward, through a small group playing a game that involved an empty fish tank and a bunch of bouncy balls, some girls singing karaoke, and a girl giving a guy a buzz cut with her eyes closed.

Lucy walked out the back door, and there were Olivia, Liza, and Gil sitting at a little table, with no one else around. For a moment she stopped and just looked at them, the three of them so luminous out there in the night. It felt like years since she'd first seen them, since this had all begun. She had a sudden urge to turn and run to her blade and never look back. But she closed her eyes and reminded herself of all those boys out there in the world whose hearts would one day be crushed by a Heartbreaker. She thought of Eleanor's sad eyes. She thought of twelve-year-old Olivia and her happy hopeful face. Lucy forced her feet forward.

"Hey," she said.

Liza looked up. "Well, well." She raised a bottle of something and took a swig.

"Hi, Luce," Gil said. "You're just in time. Olivia was just about to say something incredibly important"—she rolled her eyes—"so important she had to pull me away from a hot idiot I was about to make out with."

Olivia sipped from a bottle of water and was silent.

Lucy sat down in an empty seat, leaned forward, and took

a breath. It was now or never. "You guys, I think I found a way to make our hearts normal again." She looked down. "So we can go back to being the way we were."

No one said anything. Lucy looked up. They were all staring.

"What do you think?" said Lucy. She tried to smile. Her heart was pounding.

"Lucy," Gil said slowly. "How drunk *are you*?" And then she let out a laugh.

"I'm serious," Lucy said.

"You're telling us you figured out how we can stop being part of an ancient secret sisterhood with perfectly formed unbreakable hearts and stop being able to do *magic* for the chance to go back to the way we were before?" said Liza. "To go back to the regular boring colorless world that everyone else lives in? Oh, goody!" She clapped her hands together.

"Sign me up, please!" said Gil. "Maybe along the way we can all catch really bad cases of body lice!"

Olivia was still silent.

Lucy leaned forward. "But you don't understand. The world is only boring and colorless if you have a closed heart. If you're open, every single moment contains the possibility for something amazing."

Gil and Liza looked at each other, and this time they didn't laugh—they just shook their gorgeous heads and rolled their beautiful eyes. "Adorable sweet little Lucy," Gil said. "You've been reading too many inspirational calendars. I am seriously concerned there is something wrong with you." Gil put her head on Liza's shoulder. "Lizzie, give her some medicine."

Liza held out her drink. Lucy pushed it away. "You only feel like that because we've done too much magic already. If you would just trust . . ."

"Give it a rest," said Gil. She stood up and put one hand on her newly perfect hip. "I'm going back in. Liza, you coming?"

Liza stood. She and Gil glanced at each other and then down at Lucy. Their eyes were cold and hard, but they didn't look angry. They just looked like they were already somewhere else. And in that moment Lucy knew with horrible certainty that there would be no reaching them.

Maybe one day they'd change their minds on their own, find the truth the way Eleanor had. Only it wasn't going to happen here and it wasn't going to happen now, and there was nothing more Lucy could do. Lucy watched as Liza and Gil linked arms and walked toward the party. Olivia stood.

"Be careful," she said. "Be careful with what you're playing at."

She turned and followed Gil and Liza back toward the house. But right before she went inside, she turned back and looked Lucy in the eye, her expression intense and unreadable.

Lucy walked around the side of the house, got on her bike, and started to pedal away, legs pumping, hands tight around the handlebars. She felt herself lurching forward in the darkness. She almost fell, and panic seized her. She stopped her bike, heart pounding, and it was only then that she suddenly understood that confusing unreadable look on Olivia's face: She was afraid. And right then, Lucy knew why.

People think memory is stored in the brain. But everything that truly matters is stored in the heart.

Olivia was scared because she knew if she got her human heart back, she'd have to remember what she'd had and lost. Everything she'd been running from would catch up with her.

But if Olivia could still be afraid, then maybe it wasn't too late.

Thirty-Seven

♥

Lucy sat on Olivia's front steps, locket clasped in her fist, her entire body shaking. She wanted to get up, to pace, to do jumping jacks in the yard, but she refused to allow herself to stand, knowing if she did, there was a very good chance she'd hop on her bike and never come back.

So she sat there. And she waited. And finally Olivia's beautiful blue convertible pulled into the driveway. Lucy could hear Gil's voice as they got out of the car.

". . . our own version of the Breakies against each other," she said. "We'll break as many hearts as we can, and then, well, I don't know what. But it'll be fun, right?"

Liza laughed. "Sounds like someone's getting a little cocky now that she's so hot. Hmm?"

The three of them were right in front of Lucy now, staring at her from the bottom of the steps.

"Oh, look, Olivia," Liza said loudly. "Someone left a very strange package on your steps." She arched one perfect eyebrow.

Gil snorted, then stepped over Lucy and went inside. Liza followed. Olivia stood there staring at her.

"What are you doing here?" Olivia said.

Lucy held up the locket that she'd retrieved from Olivia's pillow. It shone in the moonlight.

"I wanted to give you this," Lucy said. A slight breeze blew and the locket swung like a pendulum.

"How did you get . . ." Olivia reached out for it as if on instinct. She grabbed it and held it in her fist. "You've been to see her, then."

Lucy nodded.

"And you don't just *think* you can get your heart back, you know you can. She told you how to do it."

Lucy nodded again. "Listen," she started to say.

Lucy heard loud voices from upstairs, the sounds of doors slamming, feet stomping.

"Lucy," Olivia said through her teeth. Her voice was a low insistent whisper. "If Gil and Liza are doing what I think they're doing, they are upstairs breaking into the tear safe." The sounds upstairs were growing louder. The voices turned to shouts. "So if you did what I think you did, you better turn and you better run like hell. . . ."

And Lucy wanted to do just that. But she would not let herself. "Come with me," Lucy said. Her heart was hammering. "We can do this together."

Olivia had opened the locket. She was staring down into it. "Why are you doing this?" It sounded like her words were strangling her. "Everything was okay, we were okay. . . ."

"That's not true," Lucy said. "And it's only getting worse." The sounds from upstairs were growing louder. "When I first met you, you told me most people don't understand all the choices that there are for the making. And you were right. But the choice isn't between being weak or strong, between being a Heartbreaker or the heartbroken. It's between following fear and following love."

Liza and Gil came barreling through the door, going so fast they were practically flying. "ALL OF OUR TEARS ARE GONE!" Gil shouted.

Liza grabbed Lucy and held on tight. Lucy tried to pull away, but she couldn't move.

"*What did you do?*" Gil said.

"Check her pack," shouted Liza. Gil tore her bag off her back and rifled through it.

"They're not here!" Gil said. "*Where did you put them,*

Lucy?" She was smiling a sickly sweet, terrifying smile.

But Lucy just shook her head. "I don't have them anymore," she said. "I . . ." She turned and tried to yank her arms from Liza's grasp. But it was no use.

Her eyes locked with Olivia's. For a moment she thought she saw her soften. *Please. Please. Please.*

But Olivia turned away.

"Bring her inside, girls," said Olivia. "If she doesn't feel like answering now, that's fine. We can wait."

Together, Liza and Gil dragged Lucy upstairs. Olivia followed.

None of them turned their heads, but if they had, they might have seen a blade of glittering swirling tears, tucked neatly into a bush next to the steps, right where Lucy had left it.

Thirty-Eight

♥

Lucy was in a small room at the end of the hallway. The room was empty except for a single hard wooden chair. She had no idea how long she'd been there, locked in that room, or how much longer she would be. "You'll stay here until you tell us where our tears are," Gil had said. "Or we figure out a way to make you." From a tiny window high up near the ceiling Lucy could see the light of the moon. It was still nighttime, at least. She wondered how long until they found the Rebreaking Blade, how long until her only chance was gone forever. She heard footsteps outside and pressed her ear against the door.

"Olivia?" Lucy said. "Is that you?"

They had been taking turns guarding the door, and no one was speaking to her, but Lucy could tell who was out there by the sound of their breath—Liza's was sharp and snarly. Gil breathed quickly and angrily. Now the breaths on the other side of the door were deep and slow, like whoever was out there was trying to quell a rising panic. This was definitely Olivia.

"I know you're scared," Lucy called out. "I know you're scared of what will happen if you get your heart back. The truth is, I cannot even imagine what it will be like to go through everything you'll have to go through. And the other truth is that using the blade isn't safe, not even a little, but there's one thing I do know for sure—if it works, you won't be alone. You'll have your grandmother, you'll have me, you'll have Pete. You'll have so many other people you haven't even met yet and an entire world to connect with. But you won't if you leave me in here and let them find the blade. This is our last chance."

Lucy stopped. "Read the letter, Olivia. Look at the locket. Please."

The only answer she got was silence, a silence so complete it was as though the person outside the room had stopped breathing entirely. But a few seconds later there was the soft *sssshk* of a lock being unlocked. And then the door opened and there was Olivia, her eyes bright, her lip quivering, her mother's locket around her neck. They stood there for a moment, perfectly still, staring at each other. And then they both began to run.

They were out in an open field with nothing but the moon, the sky, the open space. It was the perfect place to go, if you wanted to be alone. Or you didn't want anyone to hear you scream.

"Ready?" said Lucy. On the way there, Lucy had started to explain everything, but as it turned out, Olivia already knew all about it. Olivia had thought of making the blade before, had thought of doing this a million times already. But she'd been too scared, not of the possibility of death, but of the possibility of really living her life with a heart open to the world. She'd been too scared until now.

"Ready." Olivia took a breath. She looked down at the shimmering blade in her hand and then up toward the sky, toward the moon and the planets and space and her parents, whose bodies were gone but whose spirits were maybe, just maybe, somehow still out there. And in the dark, where Lucy should not have been able to see, she swore she caught Olivia smiling faintly up at the sky. And the sky smiling back down at her.

Olivia turned to Lucy. "No matter what happens, don't wait to see if I'm okay. Take the blade yourself and use it. You have to promise me, okay? The warmth of a heart melts the tears, and if you wait too long, your chance will be gone."

Lucy nodded. Olivia locked eyes with her one more time. She held the blade up to her chest. And then she smiled a tiny wry smile. "See you on the other side, honey pie."

In one swift motion, she thrust it forward and the swirling blade disappeared into her chest. Olivia opened her mouth and let out a sound, a deep, guttural, gut-wrenching howl that seemed to come not from her lips but from all around them, from all directions at once. Then she collapsed onto the ground. Lucy stared down at her. Olivia's fist uncurled, and the blade tumbled out into the grass.

Lucy picked it up. There was no time to think, there was no time to anything. Lucy pointed the blade toward her own chest, and she did not feel afraid anymore.

"Thank you," she whispered. And she sent that "thank you" out toward the sky and the earth and the trees, and toward all the magic in the world, not the spells and potions kind, but the kind that made it such that she'd ever existed at all, that she'd been able to be here and experience this and feel things, even if all too briefly. She looked out across the field for maybe the very last time, and then she closed her eyes and concentrated on all the things and people she'd ever loved. She pulled her love for them into the center of her chest; she concentrated on filling her heart up with it. One by one, she pictured their faces all in a row; one face stood out from all the others. She was ready.

With every bit of strength she had, she plunged the blade into her chest. She felt it cut through her skin, her bone, felt it touch her heart. She heard herself scream and then heard nothing at all. She collapsed into the grass and that was it.

There in that field, two girls found their hearts newly broken. And out in the world, 103 brokenhearted boys found their broken hearts magically healed.

Thirty-Nine

♥

Before her eyes were even open, Lucy heard birds, their voices sweet and high over the steady pounding of her heart. She saw the sun creeping up over the horizon, and next to her Olivia lying in the damp grass. There was blood on her T-shirt. "Olivia," Lucy whispered. "Olivia?"

Olivia blinked. Her face was streaked with tears. And as she sat up, they just kept falling. But through the tears she was smiling. "We're alive," she said.

"So we are," said Lucy. She reached up to her own face. As it turned out, she was crying too.

She brought her hand to her chest. Her heart felt tender and sore. There was blood caked on her skin but no mark where the blade had gone in. The only evidence that anything had happened was the fact that her tattoo was gone. And so was Olivia's.

Olivia scooted closer to Lucy and pulled her knees to her chest.

The two sat there together, leaning against each other. And as the sun started to rise, they turned their faces toward it. They stayed like that until it was truly, beautifully, morning.

Epilogue

Lucy wrapped her winter coat tighter around her. The icy snow crunched under her feet like sugar crystals.

"Hey, Luce!"

Lucy turned as a flutter of powder rained down on her. And there was Olivia, grinning, her cheeks flushed with cold, snow still stuck to her gloves.

"Hey, yourself!" Lucy grabbed a handful of snow with her mittens. She formed it into a ball and tossed it on top of Olivia's head. They both laughed.

"Pete wants to pick us up as soon as school ends," Olivia said. "We have to leave right away if we want to get to the cabin by sunset, which is apparently amazing from all the way up there, and there's some ice-cream place he is insisting we stop at on the way. I was like, 'Dollface, it is the day before winter break, are you out of your mind?'" She shook her head, but she was smiling. "Also, I promised Eleanor we'd stop by on the way up. She wants to meet Pete and she's excited to see you, is that okay?"

"Perfect," Lucy said. "We'll be out front."

The two girls hugged, and Lucy watched Olivia go. Off in the distance Lucy spotted two familiar figures walking toward Olivia, their gorgeous faces expressionless, their breath floating around them in great white puffs. But they passed right by her without a glance, as though she was a stranger, as though they'd never known her at all. And in their minds, they hadn't. Lucy and Olivia had been bleached from their memories, like an overexposed photograph, too bright to make out.

Lucy smiled and shook her head. It was funny how so many things had changed so quickly. For Olivia, for Eleanor. For Lucy's parents.

So many things that had once seemed very unlikely, or even completely impossible, had simply gone and happened, and were still happening. . . .

Lucy looked up. There was Tristan walking right toward her.

Their eyes met. Lucy felt warmth radiating from the center of her chest. When Tristan saw her, his lips spread into a smile. And when he was close enough, he pressed his smiling lips against hers and wrapped his arms around her waist. And then he leaned back slightly to speak. "According to Pete and the five-minute-long ice-cream-themed a cappella slash rap song he left me on my voice mail, we're only three hours away from the best ice-cream experience of our lives. He's very excited. It's pretty cute." He brought his face close to hers again. "I'll tell you what *I'm* excited about this weekend. . . ."

He let his words linger and they shared a private smile. It was different between them now, different from when they were just friends. There were times she actually felt shy around him. She'd blush sometimes when she caught him looking at her the way he did when he was about to kiss her. There was a tiny space between them now, just enough of a divide to give the sparks something to crackle across.

But there were also times they felt closer than ever. Like when they would watch the stars together from the flatbed of Tristan's truck, her head on his chest, and for a moment she'd forget that they were two separate people, she'd feel so much a part of him, and him so much a part of her.

Then again, they still had their secrets. Both of them did. And that was okay. Some of those secrets Lucy figured they'd always keep for themselves. And some would be revealed in time. This weekend she planned to show him her new tattoo. The violet, right over her heart, its purple petals open.

Someday, she might even tell him what it meant.

The bell rang. "Hey, one more thing," Tristan said. "I talked to Phee last night after she got home from going out with that guy Colin you set her up with? She was thrilled. I've never heard her like this about anyone before. She said they had an amazing time, and she thinks he's going to be her new super boyfriend forever." He paused. "How did you know they'd get along so well? I wouldn't have guessed."

Lucy shrugged. "What can I say?" she said. "I'm an incredibly gifted matchmaker." She turned to the side so he couldn't see the grin.

Tristan leaned over and kissed her on the nose. "See you later, my Lucinda," he said, then headed off to class.

And Lucy stood there for one more moment, watching her love.

Of all the things that had changed, maybe it was this that had changed most of all—her understanding of love and what it could be like. It did not give her a feeling of sick panic, this love. It was not a love that made her doubt herself nor one that she did not feel worthy of. It felt exciting and new, but warm and comforting also. It was not perfect, but it was real and it was messy, and it was beautiful in its messiness. It was not guaranteed to last forever. She knew that. Nothing was. But every moment felt so rich, so full, and she was so, so grateful for it. If it ended, then it would end. And her heart would break. But it wouldn't always be broken.

She blew a kiss toward Tristan's back, and then she pressed her hand to her chest.

Truth was, she had no idea what would happen next. And that, of course, was the point.

Acknowledgments

A huge very grateful thank-you to everyone at HarperCollins, including: Alice Jerman, Cara Petrus, Christina Colangelo, Jennifer Strada, Farrin Jacobs, Hallie Patterson, Stephanie Stein, and Melinda Weigel. Extra-special thanks to the wonderful Sarah Landis for her insightful, careful, and all-around amazing editing.

Thank you to Alyssa Reuben and Lucy Stille at Paradigm, and to Lydia Wills.

Thank you to my delightful writer friends, especially the ones with whom I discussed this book the most: Aaron Lewis, Aimee Friedman, Marpo Crosbie, Micol Ostow, Siobhan Vivian, and Susie Cavill.

And thank you to all my delightful non-writer friends.

Unlimited thanks to my parents, Cheryl Weingarten and Donald Weingarten.

Thank you so, so much to all the readers out there.

A huge thank-you to all the very fabulous bloggers who posted about *The Secret Sisterhood of Heartbreakers*, hosted contests and giveaways, ran interviews, and took the time to review the book.

And thank you to my husband, Griff.

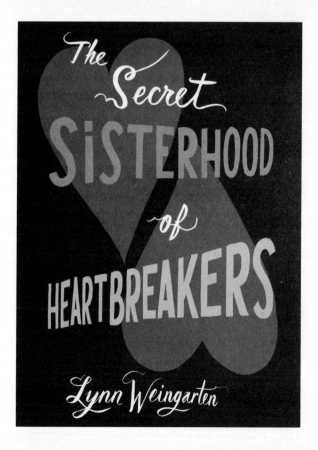